'You—' Grey took her upper arm into his free hand as he stared with aggravation, and something else that wasn't aggravation at all, right into her eyes '—are a very odd kind of personal assistant.'

She could have taken offence, but she didn't. Maybe because his fingers held her arm in a gentle clasp. He might not want to admit it, but Soph thought he found her at least a little intriguing.

His eyes widened and he stepped abruptly away from her. Soph backed towards the door. She had to put distance between them before the Gremlin of Temptation struck and she said something terribly inappropriate.

Dear Reader

Families come in all shapes and sizes. I confess I have unashamedly explored some of the motivations, behaviours and attitudes of my own broad 'family' as I've written each of my Gable sisters stories. All of that exploration is underpinned with the one special ingredient that gives us hope, holds us up and keeps us going. Love.

The Gable sisters' journey began when middle sister Chrissy Gable butted heads with Nate Barrett as she determined to protect her elderly employer from harm in HER MILLIONAIRE BOSS, and instead fell into the love of a lifetime herself. It carried through when Bella, the eldest Gable sister, and Luc Monticelli faced their combined difficult pasts in THE ITALIAN SINGLE DAD, and were finally able to find forgiveness and healing and a future together.

Now it is Sophia Gable's turn to find something even beyond the wonderful love of her sisters. And, indeed, Soph is set to take on the world, or at least the part of it populated by a certain wounded, grumbly and delicious employer named Grey Barlow—whether he thinks her quirky way of assisting and caring for him is outrageous or not! Grey is equally determined to protect himself from entanglements, but will his heart be able to resist the onslaught of one determined and unusual assistant?

I hope you enjoy Soph and Grey's story as much as I enjoyed writing it, and in this centenary year of celebrating so many wonderful Mills & Boon stories perhaps the Gable sisters will live on in your hearts just a little, as they have in mine.

Love and hugs

Jennie

THE BOSS'S UNCONVENTIONAL ASSISTANT

BY
JENNIE ADAMS

First published in Great Britain 2008
Harlequin Mills & Boon Limited,
Eton House, 18-24 Paradise Road, Richmond, Surrey TW9 1SR

ISBN: 978 0 263 86531 8

Set in Times Roman 12½ on 14½ pt
02-0808-56816

Printed and bound in Spain
by Litografia Rosés, S.A., Barcelona

Australian author **Jennie Adams** grew up in a rambling farmhouse surrounded by books, and by people who loved reading them. She decided at a young age to be a writer, but it took many years and a lot of scenic detours before she sat down to pen her first romance novel. Jennie is married, with two adult children, and has worked in a number of careers and voluntary positions, including transcription typist and pre-school assistant. Jennie makes her home in a small inland city in New South Wales. In her leisure time she loves long, rambling walks, starting knitting projects that she rarely finishes, chatting with friends, trips to the movies, and new dining experiences.

Jennie loves to hear from her readers, and can be contacted via her website at www.jennieadams.net

For Mark, because you always smile when I sing.

CHAPTER ONE

'SO THIS is where a multimillionaire property developer comes for the occasional weekend away from the city.' Sophia Gable made the observation as she drew her elderly yellow car to a stop outside Grey Barlow's country home. 'Or in this case it's where he comes to recuperate from an accident.'

The house sat part way up an unspoiled section of Victorian mountainside, a large, solid structure made of slate and stone and mortar with a weathered roof of terracotta tiles. Vines twined about the veranda posts. Meadows full of wild flowers bloomed in every direction. Beyond those, snow-capped mountains rose in early spring splendour.

It was a change from the hustle and bustle of Melbourne, but Soph was adaptable. She glanced at the white flop-eared domestic rabbit that rested, nose twitching, in a deep basket strapped to the front passenger seat of the car. Alfred might also enjoy the change of scene.

Despite Soph's efforts to remain calm, a small bout of nerves surfaced. This was a change of more than just her usual city surroundings. She sucked in a steadying breath. Her career change had been the right thing and for her first assignment she got to help a man in need, which she knew she would find fulfilling. It was all perfect. There was nothing to worry about.

Nothing except the fact that Soph had used up three of her four weeks of financial buffer zone before the We Work for You agency had given her this first posting. But the agency would see this proof of her versatility and skill and go on to send her into all sorts of varied jobs where she could help others and feel great as she did so.

Soph climbed out of the car, twitched her fluffy cerise jumper and black trousers into place and spared just a moment to admire the matching crimson ankle boots. With a cheerful expression pasted on to her face, she headed for the house and climbed the steps to the veranda.

'*You're* Sophia Gable, the assistant I acquired through the staffing agency?' The question came as a low rumble of sound from a corner of the veranda where the speaker would have had a perfect view of Gertie the Beetle's arrival, and Soph's exodus from said car. 'I thought you'd be older, less colourful.'

Was it the crimson tips in her hair? They probably

looked a bit metallic in the sunlight, now Soph thought about it, but she'd wanted power hair for this fresh start. She squinted into the shadowed corner.

'I'm Sophia, but most people call me Soph. I hope you will too, Mr Barlow.' Despite the shadows, she could make out a cast on his arm and one foot in an ankle brace, stuck out awkwardly in front of him where he sat in an outdoor chair.

Poor fellow, but at least his injuries were temporary. 'The position outline said clerical with a bit of housekeeping and cooking, other general duties and assistance related to your injuries as required. I want to assure you I'm prepared for all contingencies. I've given quite a bit of thought to how I can best assist in your recovery.'

'You can assist by performing the required tasks and driving me places when needed. I'm certain nothing else will be necessary.' He rapped the words out with every appearance of annoyance and even a hint of suspicion. 'My injuries are simple, after all.' Following this pronouncement he glared and said, 'I'm merely dealing with a sprained ankle and a broken arm. There's nothing at all to fuss about.'

'That's a very positive outlook.' Though a bit taken aback, Soph tried to put a good spin on his grouchiness. The man may have placed his injuries last on his list of needs with the agency, but they were still needs. He might require a little coaxing to accept help with them. That was all. 'Even so, I have lots of great ideas—'

'Sit down, please.' He interrupted her without compunction and gestured towards the chair opposite his. 'At least you're not late, but I don't have a lot of time for pleasantries.'

Soph moved forward and got a proper look at him. 'I thought you'd be older. It's always the way when we anticipate meeting someone, isn't it? We tend to imagine something quite different to the reality.'

She wondered what made him so defensive about his injuries, but didn't have time to think about it now.

In truth, she was a little distracted. Now she could see him properly, she acknowledged that he was rather impressively packaged. Broad-shouldered, dark-haired, he had a chiselled face and stormy green eyes and not an ounce of spare flesh on him anywhere. She'd place him in his mid-thirties.

He said in a dry tone, 'I'm sure we'll manage to get over our mutual astonishment.'

'Yes. I guess so.' Despite his dryness and his wounded irritability, he had a presence. There was something compelling about him.

Soph's pulse skittered, but she rejected her reaction. The man was a stranger, not in her social or economic set, at least a decade older than her, and her employer to boot.

When Soph chose to date, it was with average

guys her own age and financial status, and she made it clear she only wanted company for an evening out or two. If they started to want a piece of her soul or anything similar, she was out of there.

One day, a long time in the future, Soph might want to choose someone more permanent from among those very ordinary men but it would have to be a relationship she could control, and she would have to feel ready.

Something told her that Grey Barlow couldn't be ordinary or controllable if he tried. Nor did he seem the kind who would seek permanency, certainly not if it came with the picket fence she imagined she might some day want. Well, her sisters had both fallen for it.

With millionaires of their own, no less, and in spite of the trust issues they had carried, thanks to their deserting parents.

Soph hadn't suffered like Bella and Chrissy. Her older sisters had shielded her, allowed her to live a normal and happy life after their parents had abandoned them, even when things had been at their toughest. Nope. Soph had no hang-ups, just a lot of gratitude and love and the wish that she could have done more for Chrissy and Bella in return.

'I'm pleased to meet you, Mr Barlow. I hope we'll have a satisfying association while I work for you.' *This* was the point. Something new and interesting to do, something which would drive away her restlessness, give her a feeling of completion, a feeling that she had contributed in a pleasing way. She simply liked to help people, and wanted more of a chance to do so.

'The agency assured me you were the best they had to offer.' After a brief hesitation in which he lifted his right hand, frowned in annoyance and dropped it down again, he reached out his undamaged left one.

Did he have to sound so dubious about her? Soph hoped he hadn't got that impression from the agency itself. She reached out her left hand too. 'I'll do my utmost to live up to your expectations.'

The back to front handshake was firm and quickly over. It should have felt impersonal or simply awkward, but a flash of heat travelled up her arm and into her chest. She thought she saw a matching momentary reaction in his gaze.

Of course her response was a glitch, since she'd decided it wouldn't be wise to notice him in that way.

As for him, a second glance revealed nothing but a blank mask. She had probably imagined anything else.

He began to rap out words. 'On doctor's orders, I've agreed to a break here for the next week. I concede the fresh air and change of scenery probably won't do me any harm, although I think my doctor is being overly cautious about my…health.

'After the week here, I'll relocate to my town

house in Melbourne. You'll carry out your work for me at both locations.'

'I'll do my best to assist you.' The town house would have a garden, a place for Alfred's collapsible enclosure. That was a good thing. She needed to explain about Alfie, how she'd found the domestic pet abandoned, tied to a pole near her flat just last night and now needed to keep him with her.

Her employer gave a nod. 'Aside from the duties you mentioned earlier, you'll screen all my phone calls and turn away any person who might appear here at the house. I've made it clear I don't want visitors, but some people might try to ignore that fact.'

No visitors, huh? If Soph had a broken arm and a damaged ankle, her sisters and brothers-in-law would be all over her. They'd tell her how to get better, bring her food and comfort. Actually, they'd probably insist she go to live with one or the other of them until she made a complete recovery.

She wondered about Grey Barlow's family. Maybe he didn't want his work colleagues or relatives to see him at less than his best. It made a proud male kind of sense. In response to this thought, she smiled at him extra kindly. 'If anyone tries to get inside the house, I'll be better than a Pekingese. They won't know what's—'

'Bitten them?' He finished the sentence for her and a wry smile touched his lips.

'Do Pekingese bite? I think they just yap, don't they?' Soph's heart pitter-pattered. He looked younger and more approachable when he smiled. Could she be blamed for noticing? 'Do you have pets, Mr Barlow? You see, I have this—'

'No, I don't do the pet thing.' The hint of a smile disappeared, replaced by a frown. 'I'd find that kind of commitment restricting.'

Maybe she wouldn't mention Alfie's presence just yet. And definitely no picket fences on this man's horizon if he couldn't even cope with the thought of a pet responsibility. She'd been right about that, and it was fine with her.

'Perhaps we could get back to our discussion of your duties?' He sounded irritable again. 'Although I'm incarcerated here for no good reason, I concede that I can't physically cover ten floors of office space every day or go out to examine the construction sites in Melbourne and beyond until my ankle is better. But I *will* keep my finger on the pulse of the company.

'I'll keep in touch by electronic conferencing. I'll also review and respond to written reports from the various departments daily.' He paused to draw a breath. 'You'll type my correspondence and do any other work I hand over to you, including research.'

'I look forward to getting started.' Soph curved her lips into what she hoped looked a confident smile, although she began to wonder just where the 'rest' portion of his recovery came in if he planned to do all these things.

In any case, she wanted him to put his faith in her. 'I'm up for any challenge this job may represent.'

'Your positive attitude is…appreciated.' His dark gaze roved over her, lingered on the fluffy jumper, the colourful hair. It then cut to the driveway, where Gertie the faithful Beetle sat in loaded-to-the-rafters splendour.

His eyebrows lifted infinitesimally. 'You do have the skills to perform well in these areas?'

'I have proficient computer skills, I touch type at a speed of seventy-five words per minute, can format and edit any document as required and know my way around transcription machines.' It didn't matter that none of these areas had been tested beyond an evening course at the local further education college and lots of practice on the computer at home over the past months.

She'd trained for it; she was ready for it. Soph also had other skills. She hit him with all of them that she thought might be relevant. 'I understand filing systems, both on the computer and off it. I've spent plenty of time running an appointments diary and handling incoming and outgoing phone calls.' Nothing was busier than an inner city hair salon. 'My driving record is spotless.'

That last part she threw in because no doubt they'd end up going somewhere sooner or later, even if only when they moved from here to Melbourne. Backing into a pole once on her L-plates didn't count. 'Um, I've rather a lot of stuff in my car, but I'm sure I'll be able to fit your things in when it comes time for us to return to the city.'

'Your vehicle will be returned to the city for you eventually. I prefer my own car so I had a driver drop me here in it.'

Oh. Right. He'd probably sent the man back in a taxi or even had a company car and driver follow him out for the purpose. 'No problem. I enjoy the chance to drive different vehicles.'

Namely, she had driven Gertie and one other car—her brother-in-law Nate's old restored convertible, which she still remembered with fondness. She'd worn a silk scarf around her neck and big sunglasses and pretended to be a movie star, and then she'd talked her landlady into going with her and done it all again. Fun!

'I can spare you fifteen minutes to unload your belongings.' He rose to his feet and hobbled towards the front door of the house. 'Once that's done, join me in the office. It's the large room on the right as you come in. Your bedroom is upstairs, first on the left.' With those words, he tugged the door open.

It was going to be like that, was it? Come help

me, I'll even pay generously for you doing so, but don't acknowledge my injuries?

She could take care of him silently, if he wanted it that way, but Soph *would* perform all her duties to him.

'Did you bring the voice recognition software package?' He had lifted his foot off the floor, clearly because standing still on it had made it ache.

'Yes, I collected it from the agency yesterday afternoon.' She searched his face again. This time she looked beyond the appealing features to the weary lines around his eyes, the slight pallor of his face. Oh, yes. He needed to rest, get off that foot. Be pampered a little.

'Bring me the software first.' He stepped inside the door. 'I'll install it and get it going so I can at least send emails without your help and without having to type with one hand. Your first job will be the dictation I've done this morning.'

It was barely nine a.m. Soph had risen at the crack of dawn to load her car and get here on time and the man had been at work for how long already?

'I'm happy to do whatever works best for you.' Provided it included appropriate care of his injuries. She turned away and moved towards Gertie. 'I'll bring the software package straight in, then sort out everything else.'

Alfred would have to be secreted into the back garden for the moment. Soph would find the right opportunity to explain about him, but that moment didn't seem to be now. It might be a good idea to impress her employer with her dedication and hard work for an hour or two, first.

Inside the house, a phone rang.

Soph turned back. 'I'll get that for you before I start to unpack.'

She preceded him into the house and followed the ringing to its source in the office. 'Sophia Gable. Mr Barlow is unavailable at the moment. Please give me your name, phone, fax and email and the reason for your call and I'll relay it on your behalf.'

'Peter Coates here. I head up the architecture department of Barlow Enterprises.' He had a friendly voice, although right now it seemed to hold a hint of long-suffering. 'I'm returning Grey's call. He left a message saying he wanted another update on the Mitchelmore project.'

'I'll find out if Mr Barlow can speak with you.' Soph pressed the hold button and swung around.

Grey stood right behind her, closer than she had realised. Her heart did that little stutter thing again.

She thrust the phone towards him and relayed the name of the caller. 'He says you asked for another update on the Mitchelmore project. Do you want to speak to him?'

'Yes, I'll take it.' He added a muttered, 'Some

things are too important to ignore, no matter what the doctor says.'

This didn't make a lot of sense to Soph, but she placed the phone into his hand anyway.

Grey lowered himself into his office chair in a slightly awkward manoeuvre. Soph noticed that he didn't have a footrest under there or anything.

'Peter.' His attention centred immediately on his caller. 'Do you have any further news about the zoning issues?'

Soph left him to it and scuttled outside to Gertie, grabbed the software package and hurried it back into the office. Her boss still had the phone to his ear so she left the package on the desk and raced back out to the car and a problematical but adorable rabbit.

First she would take care of Alfie and then she would start to figure out how to best look after her boss.

Collapsible rabbit cage and associated paraphernalia in one hand, Alfie in his basket in the other, Soph hurried to the back of the house. She breathed a sigh of relief as she spotted a part of the garden tucked away behind a tree and a flower border, and hidden from sight of the house by a big shed that had a mesh gate enclosing its front.

'There's plenty of long grass, Alfie.' Soph tugged the collapsible enclosure upright and eased the rabbit inside, then ran to the back of the house and filled her pet's water container.

She set down the water and a bowl full of pellet supplement from the five kilogram bag she'd scrounged from a neighbour. It was just as well she knew someone with guinea pigs and that rabbits ate the same supplement. Soph placed a blanket over part of the cage for shade.

Between the friendly single mum and Joe the mechanic, who had the cage from days gone by, Soph had her bases covered. Without these things, she didn't know how she would have fed and housed Alfred, but she would have made it work somehow. She didn't walk away from anyone who needed or relied on her.

Not like her parents had done, but that was long ago.

Soph returned to the car and unloaded the remainder of her things. It took several trips. She didn't travel light and she'd brought a few things especially with her employer in mind. But she hurried, and soon presented herself in the office in time to hear Grey snarl a string of words into a headset. He then glared daggers at the resulting words as they appeared on his computer screen.

'I dropped by the kitchen. Did you want anything specific for lunch today?' A brief inventory had revealed staples—healthy enough ingredients, but nothing fancy. Fortunately, she'd brought her own extras so they wouldn't have to be bored on the food front.

Her boss drew the headphones off and tossed them on to the desk. 'You can make sandwiches or something at twelve-thirty. Meanwhile—' he gestured to the second desk '—you'll sit there. Work your way through the tapes in the order they're in the tray. You'll email the correspondence to me to look over. Once I'm happy with it, you'll fax or email each item as directed.'

'Yes, Mr Barlow.' Soph took the first tape and fitted it into the player on the second desk but she didn't immediately sit down.

'Grey will do.' He turned away, retrieved his headset and started to growl again. He interspersed the words with occasional irritated clicks of his computer mouse and one-handed typing.

It seemed the new voice program and he hadn't fully come to an understanding as yet.

Soph left the room, pulled a soft scatter cushion from one of the big squishy chairs in the living room and carried it back into the office. She grabbed two reams of copy paper from a box in the corner and, armed with packets of paper and cushion, dropped to her hands and knees beside his desk and edged underneath. 'Okay, I'm ready. Lift your foot and I'll scoot all this under.'

He didn't respond immediately and Soph wiggled

a little. The floor felt hard beneath her knees, despite the curves on the rest of her.

A hiss of breath followed and then some muffled words that sounded like, 'Anything to get you out from under there.' He lifted his foot.

Soph gently moved the paper packages and cushion into place. 'Try that and let me know if it's soothing at all.'

'Soothed is not the word that comes to my mind right now.' He spoke in a controlled tone that, oddly, sent delicious warmth in a cascade down her spine. But he lowered his foot.

When he said nothing more, Soph assumed all was well—the first strike at looking after him went to her. She wiggled out from under the desk and got to her feet, dusting her trouser legs although she suspected a cleaner had been through here recently.

'I'd be happy if you'd place your bottom in your chair now, Sophia, and keep it there.' His eyes glittered and he seemed to almost grind his teeth before he looked away. 'Quite a lot of that correspondence is urgent.'

Soph stared at the back of his beautifully shaped head as sensual awareness belatedly impinged on her consciousness. Heat rushed into her face. *That* was the reason for his indrawn hiss of breath a moment ago? He'd been watching her bottom wiggle?

With a muttered agreement, Soph hurriedly took up her workload.

CHAPTER TWO

AS THE hours passed Soph learned a number of things. Her new employer knew how to churn out work. The phone wasn't about to stop ringing simply because she needed to concentrate, and Grey had three stepmothers who all seemed determined to demand his attention. *Three!*

At twelve-thirty Soph handed her boss the latest phone message, from Leanna Barlow:

'I'm his stepmother, dear. I hope he's feeling all right? Good, good. I also need to touch base with him and…um…talk to him about a little problem I have with my credit cards…'

The message followed similar ones from Sharon Barlow and Dawn Barlow, who had both bemoaned Grey's absence from Melbourne and his idea that he should isolate himself completely in the country for the first phase of his recovery.

They had then said they respectively wanted to—Sharon—use his yacht for a three-month cruise and—Dawn—use the plane the company chartered to fly to Greece because there was this expo on for the next week and a half—something to do with hand-crafted table decorations.

Grey ignored all the messages and carried on with his work.

Soph wanted to get chatty and ask about his family, but refrained. She did, however, help herself to a piece of paper she spotted tucked half under a pile of files on his desk as she stood there after passing him the latest message.

'Is this your physio outline?' Exercises he hadn't done all morning? 'I can help you with the routine now. It's lunch time, so we're due for a break anyway.'

'I'll do the exercises before I join you for the meal.' He held his hand out for the piece of paper. 'That will give you time to organise some food.'

Soph pretended not to notice his outstretched hand and, instead, walked to the photocopier in the corner of the room and made a copy of the regimen. She then passed the original back to him and disappeared into the kitchen with her page before he could say anything. She studied it as she went.

While the soup heated, Soph rushed out to the back garden via the laundry room door. Alfie was fine, but clearly wanted to play, and to come back inside with her. When she spoke his name—made up when she'd found him because she'd thought he looked like an Alfred and he had had no identification on him—he twitched his nose as though he liked to hear it.

Soph smiled at the thought and gave him as much time as she dared, then returned inside alone. It still didn't seem a good idea to bring the topic of the rabbit up with her boss.

Grey hobbled into the kitchen moments after she got there.

'The food is almost ready.' She gestured towards the table. 'Please, have a seat.'

He sniffed the air. 'What can I smell? Sandwiches would have done. There's shaved double-smoked ham in the fridge, cheese, pickles.'

'It's soup. I made it last night.' Her sisters said her cooking efforts were legendary for all the wrong reasons. Her brothers-in-law agreed, but Soph thought they all just liked to tease her.

After all, she ate her creations and couldn't discern anything wrong with them. 'I hope you like roast pumpkin with some other vegetables blended in. I've flavoured it with curry paste, Italian herb blend and vanilla bean. I'll make toasted sandwiches to follow.'

'I see.' He lowered himself into a chair and again his weariness showed. 'It sounds…interesting.'

'Yes, exactly. Spices add variety to life,' she said, deliberately rewording the usual saying and smiled at him, then carried the mugs of soup to the table and placed one in front of him before she took her seat opposite. 'You need good food to help you get well.'

'Healthy food and quiet surroundings, fresh air and rest and a complete break from all stressors.' Her employer seemed to quote the words verbatim. No doubt the admonitions had come from his doctor, although it did sound a little over-the-top for these simple injuries.

Grey certainly should get some rest, though, yet had he slowed his workload? If he had, she hated to imagine what it was like normally.

Lips pursed, he took a tentative sip of the orange brew. His nose wrinkled and he sniffed it a second time. Another sip followed, and he frowned and poured himself a glass of water from the jug on the table and quickly drank.

'I'm glad you understand the concept of rest to help you get better.' Even if he wasn't following it very well as far as she could see.

He gave her a sharp glance across the table, but Soph maintained a serene, silent pose. Her boss may not realise it yet, but he really did need her. To chivvy him along, watch out for him.

With a smile still hovering, Soph tasted the soup. Oh, yes, lovely job. She lifted her gaze and waited, eyebrows raised, for him to express his opinion.

Grey cleared his throat. 'You say you made the soup yourself, especially to bring here?'

'Yes. Last night. It took a couple of hours, but I wanted to get you off to a good start, and I figured there might not be time to make it today once I got here.' She had certainly been right about that.

His shoulders shifted in a gesture that seemed to reflect a mental discomfort rather than a physical one. Then, with a deep breath, he raised his soup mug and drank it all down. His eyes sparkled and a flush rose in his cheeks as he set the mug back on the table.

Sunshine broke out all over Soph's world. She had harboured just the tiniest seed of doubt, but he didn't know about that and had gulped her food with alacrity anyway.

'*You liked it.*' Pleasure and a hint of gratitude filled her voice. Grey Barlow liked her soup! Soph buried her nose in her mug to hide her grin.

'It was…very tasty.' He drank more water.

The water would also benefit him. Soph nodded her approval. Somewhere sweet and warm inside her couldn't help but soften towards him. They had tastes in common—culinary ones at least—even if he felt a little shy about expressing his compliments to her.

Well, it was probably fine to like him, provided none of those other initial responses resurfaced.

When they finished the toasted sandwiches minutes later, she turned a determined gaze on him. 'It's time to do the physio exercise you can't do by yourself. I've looked at the sheet and, if you don't do it, you'll miss one of the most helpful exercises on the list. You did do the rest, didn't you?'

'I did, and it's not convenient to do more right now. I have work waiting.' His lips stopped just shy of a manly pout. 'Besides, I've already replaced the brace and laced it up.'

'You shouldn't have done that, either.' Soph got to her feet and *did not* think about how kissable his lips might be, shaped in just that particular way.

He wasn't at all adorable in his prickly splendour, either. He was stubborn and far too protective of his personal space when he'd hired her to get right in it. That was the fact of the matter. 'Not unless you tied the laces one-handed.'

She searched the kitchen drawers until she found a cloth long enough to suit her purposes. 'Shall we go? You said you're in a hurry.'

On those words she bustled into the sitting room before he could argue and hoped he would simply follow. The boss-man needed a little bossing of his own.

'Why don't you sit there, on the sofa?' Sophia gestured without looking at Grey, for all the world as though she hadn't just ordered him about in his own home. Albeit a second home he visited less often than he would like, when he managed to eke out some free time to climb in the nearby mountains.

Grey wasn't accustomed to taking orders. He wasn't accustomed to having his statements ignored, either. He wanted to be able to scale those mountains too, not be stuck just looking at them when he glanced out of the windows. 'I did say I don't have time for this.'

'I know, but we're here now and it will only take a couple of minutes.' She blinked guileless sherry-coloured eyes at him.

The lashes were ridiculously long. If he held her to him, cheek to cheek, those lashes would brush his skin. 'Fine, do your worst. Just get on with it.'

'First I'll have to unlace the ankle brace and remove it.' She waited expectantly.

Grey sat. Controlling her was like trying to trap light in a bottle. He had no idea how to manage her exuberance.

Sophia sat beside him, so close their thighs pressed together. Necessary, he knew, but the knowledge didn't stop him from tensing as his body catalogued every nuance of that touch, reacted to it and wanted more of it.

She had golden skin and a soft, slender neck, her face a perfect oval with winged brows and a straight little nose and full, generous lips that were right out of a man's fantasy. His gaze caught on those lips, caught on the smile that lingered there even now.

With a murmured word, Sophia leaned down and

made quick work of removing the brace. When finished, she turned that megawatt smile on him again. The breath she drew held just enough of a hitch to tell him she wasn't unaware of their closeness.

'There.' She lifted her hand and almost patted his leg. Almost, before she snatched her wandering appendage back. 'The brace is off. Let's get started with the exercise, shall we?'

'By all means, let's complete the physio routine.' Grey didn't want assistance with his physiotherapy. He didn't want to be incarcerated in the countryside for the next week either, but Doc Cooper had some bug in his brain that Grey could be on the road to serious trouble.

All because a few readings had come in high on the scale after the accident—it was silly! Just because Grey's mother had died young of a heart attack, no apparent trigger, and his father had had high cholesterol and high everything else before he, too, had died.

Okay, those weren't silly, but *Grey* looked after himself. 'Bloody doctor probably doesn't know what he's on about, anyway.'

'Your exercises seem sensible to me,' Sophia offered with a slightly confused look.

Grey ignored it and instead noted the way her hair cupped her face and neck.

Her body was all sweet curves. The sight of her

bottom as it had wiggled about beneath his desk had almost made him moan, and Grey wasn't someone to be affected easily by a woman.

Not unless he chose to be, and never involuntarily. Yet he'd noticed Sophia.

'How does that feel?' Her mouth formed the words and Grey could imagine her lips beneath his, lush and generous.

He didn't want to, damn it.

Because Sophia Gable wasn't only fluffy and colourful and capable of making a soup that truly defied description; she was a girl some man would take home to his mother. Grey didn't take women anywhere, other than to bed. He stayed away from the kind who wouldn't understand that.

As for the idea of him taking a woman to meet his three stepmothers? What a concept.

'Grey? Your foot?' Sophia spoke as though to prompt a child. 'I'm trying not to hurt you.'

'You're not hurting me, and you won't.' Injuries aside, she had no power to hurt him in other ways. No woman did. Grey had seen to that, yet he wondered at his need to voice the knowledge aloud. Another thought followed.

He could hurt Sophia Gable without trying.

Grey was a hard man, toughened by years in a cutthroat business world. Hardened by his upbringing, too, although that truly was history, aside from the ongoing legacy of his late father's three bored and at times self-indulgent past wives. He had let himself love them as surrogate mothers, one after another, until he'd finally realised the futility and refused to love anyone at all.

Sophia Gable was too gentle for him, soft and young. She looked as though she would care about anyone who gave her half a chance, and would expect them to care for her in return. Such women were made for marriage—an institution Grey respected when it worked, but would never enter into.

Why hadn't he dismissed her completely from his awareness, then? Why did the curiosity, the interest, remain?

'I appreciate your trust in me.' She misread the meaning behind his words. Luminous eyes smiled at him. 'My middle sister Chrissy broke two toes once, when we decided to rearrange the furniture in our apartment and she didn't have her glasses on.'

A chuckle escaped. 'That was a few years ago, but boy, did Bella, the eldest, get uptight. We all live separately now, but we had some fun times.'

For a moment he thought she looked just the tiniest bit sad, but she went on to work on his ankle, and to prattle about her life in Melbourne, and the thought faded.

A picture of a close-knit family emerged. Two elder sisters, one with a stepdaughter, the other with a nine-month-old baby named Anastasia. The husbands of those sisters. An elderly grandfather they all seemed to have taken to their hearts.

How would it feel to have a family like that? Grey couldn't begin to imagine. He realised her chatter had died away and she had released his ankle.

'Are you done already?' The woman had talked to distract him while she'd put him through the requisite number of stretches. It had worked, and they'd been perfectly undisturbed the whole time. He even felt something close to relaxed—almost sleepy, actually.

Doc Cooper would be pleased.

Grey shuffled the sarcastic thought aside. He had goals to focus on. 'It's a wonder the phone hasn't rung several times by now.'

'It probably has. I put it on silent ring and sent it to the answering service before I left to make our lunch.' She didn't lift her head as she replaced and laced the exoform brace.

His relaxed mood frayed. 'I need to know of all incoming phone calls the moment they occur. I have a company to control.' He leaned forward and gave her the benefit of his displeased expression. 'There could have been something urgent.' One project in particular had issues right now and could cost him upward of three million dollars if it crashed and burned.

Her gaze locked with his, caught in the glare of his

anger. 'I'm sorry. I thought lunch time would be a break from all of that. I'll check the messages now.'

The woman sounded disappointed in herself and her mouth looked vulnerable, as it had when she'd watched and waited to see if he liked her bizarrely flavoured soup. It might have grown on him, he supposed, but how could he know for certain? His taste buds had imploded after the first two sips.

Another urge overcame Grey now. For a scant moment in time, he thought of kissing her uncertainties away. Maybe he revealed something of that thought as he looked at her because her gaze flared from curiosity to interest.

Of its own volition, Grey's body leaned towards hers. She copied his action before she stopped abruptly.

'I'll turn the coffee on to brew before I check the messages. I prepared it earlier so it's only a matter of flicking a switch.' She removed herself from beside him, didn't stop until she stood half a room away.

With her hands clasped in front of her she cleared her throat. 'I assume you'd like coffee?'

'One cup.' Damn the doctor's orders. 'Not too strong, plenty of milk.' Grey forced aside other wants—unacceptable wants that had nothing to do with coffee. It must be the country air addling his brain. Not that he'd breathed any of it except for this morning when he'd waited those few minutes on the veranda for Sophia to arrive.

Well, country air or simply the closeness of a woman—he had reacted on instinct, no thought involved. Now he had to engage his brain to override those instincts. Sophia Gable was not someone he should mess with.

'You could take a nap instead of going straight back to work.' She fidgeted from one foot to the other, burned into action, perhaps, by his glare.

'I'm keeping off the foot as much as I can.' Yes, he'd felt better, but, considering his injuries, that was to be expected. 'And I'll turn in at a decent hour tonight.' Those were the only concessions he would give, and 'decent hour' was a relative term.

She sighed. 'Coffee it is, then.'

Soph did indeed sigh, and repeated the sigh as she hesitated before she left the room. She didn't want to irritate her employer, truly she didn't. Rather, she wanted to help him, to be of assistance, to contribute appropriately to the working relationship. He didn't make that easy. Nor did the way she reacted when in close proximity to him.

'Are you resting well at night?' She tried not to picture him in that big bed in the master suite and, yes, she had peeped into the room when she'd first arrived. So sue her.

Grey shook his head, whether as a statement of his lack of rest or resistance to her questions, she couldn't have said. 'Perhaps we should concentrate on you, Sophia, and your tendency to make arbitrary decisions about my care without consulting me.' He got to his feet. 'I'm not accustomed to that kind of behaviour in my employees.'

'I won't do the phone thing again.' Why did she get all shivery when he put on his growly voice? She pushed the question aside. Maybe it was simply chilly today or something.

And he was annoyed with her. She should think about *that*. 'You see, I thought you wanted me to take care of all those things, but that you didn't want either of us to acknowledge my efforts openly.'

When he didn't appear to understand, she went on. 'I thought your pride was stung and, although that would actually be silly, I would still be willing to work with it but you would have to reciprocate. I must be able to take proper care of you.'

Her voice tightened at the end of that statement, because it mattered, blast him. She wanted to succeed at the job. And yes, fine, maybe she also needed to feel useful and know she was giving back, not just receiving. It was called a community consciousness, and lots of people had it.

Certainly it was nothing to do with him personally, or with the fact that he attracted her just a little.

She turned her focus back to what mattered, and cut him a glare to make it clear she meant business right now. 'The alternative is that I do nothing at all for you. That's not acceptable to me.'

'I'm not embarrassed by my injuries.' Even as he said it, a faint tinge of colour came into his cheeks.

Soph raised her gaze farther and got caught in deep-green eyes that seemed to hold surprise, a hint of unease, and something else.

'I'll play back the phone messages while you make the coffee. If anything's gone amok, I'll just have to fix it.' Most of his anger was gone now.

She was glad that he was prepared to let the matter go.

The deep mellow tone of his voice raised goose flesh on her skin despite the distance between them, despite her lofty resolutions. That wasn't so great.

As though he, too, felt it, he shook his head. 'Take a few minutes to pre-plan what we'll eat for dinner tonight.' Oh, prosaic words, but his gaze held a different story. 'Perhaps a casserole, so it can cook while we work.' He made his suggestion without meeting her gaze. 'There's a pre-set function on the oven.'

Broad shoulders and slender hips receded from her view while Soph stood there, silent. She told herself to wake up, stop watching, to resist the lure of an interest that couldn't be allowed to grow.

Already she liked him, was intrigued by him, felt more towards him than she should. That had to stop.

Grey buried himself in work for the rest of the afternoon. He seemed intent on maintaining distance. Those two things were good, Soph decided as she clacked away on the computer keyboard and assured herself that that earlier aberration of feeling *was* now firmly in the past.

While Grey scattered his emails about the universe, Soph worked her tail off on his tapes.

'I need to check on the casserole now.' She took a deep breath and suggested he sit on the veranda in the sunshine. 'It won't last much longer, and Vitamin D is good for you. Or is it Vitamin E? Whichever is right, just give it ten minutes. That's all I'll need, and I'll bet it makes you feel good.'

He muttered under his breath as he hobbled out there, taking his dictation recorder with him, but he went. Soph managed the food issues in seven minutes and spent the other three with a lonely and disgruntled Alfie.

'Taking a "smoko" break?' Grey asked from the kitchen when she rushed back inside. She almost jumped out of her skin.

'I'm certainly not. I don't do that. That is, my sisters would have flayed me if I'd ever decided to try it, and once I grew up I didn't want to anyway.'

She snapped her jaws shut before any more babble could escape.

'I just took a breath of fresh air.' Soph sidled inside. He couldn't have seen Alfie's cage, even if he had looked all the way through and out the laundry room door. She moved to step past him and return to the office. 'You don't smell cigarette smoke on me, do you?'

What a dumb question. Did she want him to grab her and sniff her hair, her clothing? Not to mention that would be far too close for comfort—witness the problems she'd had after lunch when she'd helped him do ankle stretches.

'You smell like flowers,' he pronounced and turned his back and started towards the office once more. 'I don't need to get close again to know that.'

Well, certainly not, and no doubt he didn't *want* to get close, either. She was simply the hired help, and short-term help at that.

So not in his league, Sophia.

He wasn't in hers, either.

Nope. Grey Barlow was not ordinary, not a safe bet.

Yet he had noticed the subtle scent she wore. Soph had only dabbed the tiniest bit behind each ear and on her wrists before she'd left home this morning.

So what? She had simply leaned too close to him on the sofa. He couldn't help but smell her perfume, and probably didn't even like it.

'The casserole is doing nicely.' She needed to get back to matters at hand. 'It's a curry, since you enjoy spicy food. I'll serve rice pilaf with it.' As though he would even care, but the silence yawned and Soph talked on. 'You…you smell quite nice, yourself.'

That stopped her, even if it was a little late. With a sharp breath she bustled past him and subsided into her office chair. From then on she focused her attention on her work!

She did, however, draw the line at six o'clock. With a determined air she shut down her computer and tidied the remaining work on her desk. Then she faced her employer and waited until he gave up on whatever he was typing one-handed and lifted his head reluctantly to look at her.

'It's after six o'clock. You must have worked since at least seven this morning to churn out so many tapes before I got here. That's an eleven hour day and far more than you should take on.

'Would you like your bath before or after dinner, and would you like me to shut down your computer for you while you make your way to the living room and start your next set of physio exercises?' She asked it all in one stream of words and then waited, arms crossed in front of her.

'There's still work for me to do before I finish for the day.' He gestured towards the computer screen.

'I think your company can probably survive

without your input until tomorrow morning.' Most of the employees would have gone home by now, wouldn't they? 'Unless you work your people in around-the-clock shifts, none of this is going anywhere at this hour, anyway.'

'Be that as it may…' he started.

'I'll just help you with this.' Soph leaned across, saved his email into his drafts folder, clicked out of the program and shut his computer off.

He made a half startled, half disbelieving sound and pushed his chair back. It had the unfortunate result that his shoulder brushed against the inside of her outstretched arm and across her breast.

Soph froze. He froze. And then they both hurriedly shifted away from each other.

He got to his feet, swung to face her, wincing as he did so, and the movement put pressure on his ankle. He cradled his arm against his body.

Irritated green sparks shot at her from his eyes.

'Don't bother to say anything.' She held up her hand. 'You left me no other choice.'

Had the man heard of backing off a little, rather than needing to be right in the thick of everything that happened in his working world? Yes, he appeared to have a project in trouble, but what about all the reports that things were going perfectly well in other departments? Did he really need to be so hands-on and go into such detail with all of that?

Soph poked a finger into the air in front of him. 'Your ankle is causing you pain. For the last two hours you've favoured your arm. I suspect it should be in a sling, but would you answer me when I asked about either of those things earlier? No. I got the death glare while you continued to speak into Bear Growling.'

'Bear Growling?' He stepped closer until they were almost nose to nose.

The intensity in his gaze made her catch her breath. 'I...uh...it's how I think of your voice program.'

Because he had a gorgeous growly voice that she would like to listen to, snuggled at his side...

No. She wanted no such thing.

Irritation crept through his tone even now. 'It's not my fault the voice program doesn't work properly. I trained it at the start, exactly as instructed.'

'Yes, but did you snarl at the time, because if you didn't, it wouldn't recognise snarl-speak now, would it?' Soph said absently, still caught in the thought of having him growl just for her. When she realised what she had said and glanced at his face, she almost laughed at the look of surprise there.

'You—' he took her upper arm into his free hand as he stared with aggravation and something else that wasn't aggravation at all, right into her eyes '—are a very odd kind of personal assistant.'

She could have taken offence but she didn't.

Maybe because his fingers held her arm in a gentle clasp and stroked lightly. The bear might not want to admit it, but Soph thought he found her at least a little intriguing.

His eyes widened and he stepped abruptly away from her. Soph backed towards the door. She had to put distance between them before the Gremlin of Temptation struck and she said something terribly inappropriate. Like, Grey, I really notice you as a man even though I've decided it's not a good idea to do so, and it's clear you're appalled that you've noticed me.

Instead, Soph went for the most prosaic words she could come up with. 'Will you come into the kitchen? I'll tape a bag over your cast so it doesn't get damaged if you accidentally splash it while you're bathing.' She blocked her mind to all thoughts of her employer in the bathtub!

'I'll cope without a bag on the arm.' He just said so instantly, unequivocally, and turned away.

Soph didn't feel the least disappointed in this further example of his resistance to her care. The attraction side of it was irrelevant, of course. Hmph. But what could she do if he wouldn't accept her help?

'I'll get on with dinner, then. I still have a side dish to prepare to go with the curry.' She turned her back, busied herself in the kitchen and didn't look around again until she heard water running upstairs. At least she had the healthy food aspect well in hand.

Soph donned protective mitts and drew the casserole out of the oven, removed the lid, then discarded the mitts and gave the contents of the dish a vigorous stir.

She and her employer just had some random chemical reaction going on between them. No doubt it would go away through lack of a receptive audience. On either side!

CHAPTER THREE

'Oh, good, you're ready for me. It seems I've timed it exactly right.' Soph pushed the door to her employer's bedroom wider and stepped through the aperture. They'd eaten their dinner. Afterwards Soph had suggested they watch some television together and had received a blank look followed by a resistant one before Grey had said he had business phone calls to make, excused himself and disappeared into the office.

At least he'd seemed to somewhat enjoy chatting with her over the meal. Not that Soph had *needed* him to enjoy her company. Nor had she been overly conscious of her boss in the short time they'd spent together. She had worked on her silly, earlier inappropriate awareness of Grey and had that all under control now.

'Let me put this tray down and I'll help you get settled in the bed.'

The tray held a ceramic incense burner complete with stand, candle holder and tiny teapot on top, matches and a drinking mug full of steaming liquid. In a trice she placed the tray on to the dresser and turned to face her boss.

Nurse Sophia to the rescue.

Her employer hovered, features frozen, near his bed. He wore green silk pyjama trousers and, well, nothing else actually, which meant Soph had a rather amazing view of his broad shoulders, his chest, the smattering of hair that tapered towards his navel…

'Ah, it's warm in here, isn't it?' Soph snapped her gaze upward, away from silk, away from his chest, though meeting his gaze wasn't particularly better. Did he have to look so *sensual* to go along with his air of fierce affront?

'I can't say I'd noticed any particular warmth,' he snarled, but he also examined her from her hair—piled in a loose, messy knot on top of her head—to her face, her mouth and finally over her body and back up again. His muscles tensed.

Soph wanted to touch him.

No. Soph did *not* want to touch him.

'Um, well, you probably put out a lot of body heat.' She waved vaguely towards him. 'Hence no need for a shirt to wear to bed.'

A shirt she truly had expected to see on him when she barged in to settle him down for the night. Nurse Sophia, indeed. If she got much hotter from looking at him, *she* would become a medical emergency.

Temperature far too hot, Doctor. What should we do?

'Why are you here?' Grey's eyes flared for just a moment before he snapped his gaze away from her. When he turned back, the irritation had returned in full force. His eyebrows drew down and a muscle twitched at the base of his jaw. 'I told you when I stepped out of the office that I planned to retire for the night.'

'Yes, so I came to help.' She'd been finished with the telly anyway. Soph tried not to look back at his chest, but it was so…*there*. And he *had* looked at her with interest before he'd locked the reaction down.

In the same way Soph needed to reject it. That was the thing. She couldn't afford to desire her boss, and he clearly didn't want to desire her.

'I'm here to work,' she blurted. 'I mean, I'm here to work in your room, to put you to bed. I took a shower, gave you time to do whatever it is you might have needed to do, and then came to help you get settled. That's why I'm in my nightwear. It seemed silly to dress again.'

It didn't seem silly now, but it was too late. She reached for the incense burner and matches, clutching them tightly because he just might see her hands shaking if she didn't.

He sent an incredulous stare her way. 'You came to help me get settled, in my room, without even knocking first.' He waved his hand towards her. 'Wearing…a hibiscus caftan and bare feet and who knows what underneath? Did it occur to you I might be buck naked in here?'

Grey Barlow.

Naked.

In this bedroom with the great big bed.

I am not seeing those things in my head…

Anyway, the caftan covered a perfectly respectable tank top and pyjama bottoms. Lots of layers really, even if Soph felt as though he'd just swept his hands along the length of her bare skin.

'The door was partly open. I don't think you'd have left it that way if you were…if you weren't…um…adequately attired.'

This said, she stepped forward and whipped the bedcovers out of the way with her free hand. 'In you get. You'll be so pleased with what I've brought for you.'

There. They could get back to business now.

Except he didn't move.

Soph plumped his pillows and patted the mattress. 'I'll take the ankle brace off once you're settled.' Perhaps he would feel more comfortable if she busied herself while he got in? She turned aside, set the burner down on his bedside table, lit the candle and positioned the unit just so.

Her employer clamped a wad of the covers into

his fist and climbed into the bed, where he promptly propped himself against the headboard. 'You can remove the brace and then remove yourself. I don't need a nanny.'

He yanked the covers across as much of him as he could while still leaving his ankle exposed. 'What is that thing, anyway? A miniature fondue set or something?'

'It's an incense burner. I've put some lovely forest-scented oil in the water. You'll find it relaxing.' As she spoke, she perched on the bed beside him, batted his hands away from where he was tugging at the laces on his brace and finished the job for him in a far gentler manner. 'And I'm not "nannying" you, I'm doing my job.'

Only her job and nothing more, even if she had slipped just a little when she'd first stepped into the room.

'The incense will help you sleep, and so will this.' Soph went to the tray again and returned with the steaming cup in her hands. She sat and held it out to him.

His fingers wrapped around the cup, brushing hers.

'It's chamomile tea.' Hopefully, he would doze off and stay asleep until morning. Hopefully, he wouldn't realise that just a touch from him put a flame to all her nerve endings and hung doubt above her determination to ignore her interest in him. 'If you're in pain, though, you must tell me. Do you have some painkillers? I can bring you water…'

'The ankle is uncomfortable.' His lashes swept down to conceal his eyes. After a cautious sniff, he took a sip of the tea and then he shrugged his shoulders, a ripple of bone and sinew and flesh that she tried not to see, not to think about. 'That's all.'

'I'm glad it's tolerable. And…ah…I've just realised I've forgotten one part of my—' *care package* '—um…of what I meant to bring in. Drink the tea and wait right here.' She hurried down the hallway and returned a moment later with a heart-shaped cushion. 'My sister Chrissy swore by one of these during her pregnancy. I think it will be perfect for your ankle at night.'

'I really don't want a bright fluffy cushion.' He cast a look of distaste towards the offending article.

Soph almost relaxed in the face of that look. It was the usual grumpy Grey. Except that his gaze, when he returned it to meet hers, was not truly grumpy, but deep and green and reluctantly but insistently interested. In her. Not in a cushion.

'You should leave—'

'Ah, well, I'll just—'

They both stopped.

Soph lifted the covers to slip the cushion under his foot. Her hands barely trembled at all and she managed a fair simulation of calm cheerfulness when she pointed out, 'The cushion isn't fluffy, anyway. Although I concede it is quite a bright yellow. I bought it to match my car, you see.'

'Yes, I think I do see. You are, though, fluffy and bright.' He placed the half empty teacup on his bedside table next to the incense burner. The scent of forest wafted around them. 'Fluffy jumpers, bright hair, a megawatt smile that makes a man want—'

He didn't end the thought. Instead, his gaze narrowed. He gestured beyond her, to the laptop computer propped against the wall. 'You should go to bed, get some rest. You're so young. The long day has probably exhausted you. If you wouldn't mind, now I'm settled here…'

'I don't mind at all.' Soph knew what he wanted—his laptop so that he could continue to work into the night.

He also wanted her out of the room because he didn't desire her—not really, not rationally. She wanted all this distraction over with as much as he did. She did! And he'd just told her she was a baby. Her eyes narrowed.

She stifled the urge to repudiate his statement, though, because he didn't look at her as though he found her immature.

Not a particularly helpful observation, Soph!

She rose from the bed and reached for the laptop. 'The candle will burn out after about an hour, so you don't need to worry about it starting a fire in the house or anything. I'll be busy downstairs for a while but if you have any urgent needs just yell and I'll come to you straight away.'

She took the empty tray in one hand and his laptop computer in the other and moved to the door quickly enough that he didn't have time to realise her intention until it was too late.

With one finger she flipped off his light and then stepped through the door. 'I'll leave the laptop downstairs for you so it'll be there first thing in the morning. No trouble at all—I'm glad you thought of it and asked me. Peaceful dreams to you.'

Soph closed the door and high-tailed it downstairs, telling herself to be relieved to be away from a temptation named Grey Barlow.

Once he got over her taking his laptop away Soph would return to her room. She would sneak a certain rabbit in with her, but Grey had finished work for the night, whether he liked the fact or not. If he followed her downstairs to try to get his laptop back, she would tell him so.

Was Soph finished being attracted to him?

She should be, but she couldn't say she was. She would have to work on that, get her defences raised properly, and how hard could it be, even though it had proved difficult just now? She'd never had this problem before!

* * *

Grey had fallen asleep as he'd waited for Sophia to return up the staircase so he could demand his laptop computer back. Sassy piece of work—and he wasn't referring to the laptop. He'd wanted Sophia to stay, sit on the edge of his bed and talk to him.

That wasn't all he had wanted, though. They had both known that and so he had called her a child, even though she wasn't and his body had been insisting he take her in his arms and treat her in a very womanly way indeed.

He had told her to leave and for her own reasons she had also decided to go. It had been best.

Grey didn't want to know those reasons so he could demolish them. She seemed to sense that he wasn't the right kind of match for her anyway. Clever girl.

No, clever woman, because even if young and sweet and perhaps a little naïve in her determination to care for him, no matter what he wanted, she *was* all woman.

He muttered a growl. He *had* slept, too. All the way through, for the first time since he'd lost his footing at the rain-washed construction site and tumbled and tumbled to fall in an ignominious heap and be carted off in a blasted ambulance despite his protestations.

Perhaps her incense and yellow cushion hadn't been so silly. But there were limits. He must control Sophia Gable so she gave him the assistance he had in mind, not her brand of it. And he would oust the stubborn attraction to her that didn't want to die.

He would oust this temporary stress level nonsense, too. He swilled down the blood pressure pills with a grimace and swore he'd be off them again in no time. They were an overreaction on the doctor's part anyway.

The doctor would test his levels again at his check-up, see the readings had been anomalous, probably due to the accident itself, and declare Grey fit again.

With a decisive nod, he moved out of his *en suite* bathroom and headed downstairs, ankle brace in hand. He'd heard Sophia open the back door of the house earlier, so he knew she was up.

Despite himself, a sense of anticipation rose as he approached the kitchen. What interesting food might she have concocted for their breakfast? What might she be wearing today? Last night's curry had been death-defying, quite exhilarating, actually, and very, very tasty once he'd got over the initial burn and the unusualness of it and had suppressed the urge to cough until he was red in the face and gasping.

'You're getting bored, old man. Some might even say pathetic.' He muttered the words in disgust. Infatuated with what his assistant cooked and wore? Her food would probably give him ulcers or, at the least, permanent tastebud damage, and her clothing was so bright he needed sunglasses to look at her.

Maybe he was simply infatuated, full stop.

Grey cast that thought aside. He didn't do infatuation. He made choices in favour of carefully thought out short-term liaisons with no emotions involved.

Yes. On that thought he stomp-hobbled into the kitchen. He would grump his interest in her to a quick death. She might dislike him for it, but that was a small price to pay to make them both forget any attraction they might have felt. He blithely ignored the fact that he had been grumpy since Sophia had arrived and it hadn't seemed to put her off all that much.

'You confiscated my laptop last night.'

'Good morning. You're up. Did you sleep well?' She swung around, searching his face while colour crept into her cheeks. It revealed both her guilt and her consciousness of him, and it rattled Grey's composure far more than he would have thought possible.

They weren't doing that any more. He'd decided. He had attacked her verbally to ensure there were no reminders. He growled some more. 'Don't ignore what I said.'

'I'm not.' Her face shone with good humour and a hint of mischief, just as though she didn't care less about his grouchiness. In fact as though she enjoyed it, which wasn't exactly what he'd set out to achieve. She couldn't *like* him being grumpy?

How did this one bright, fluffy woman manage to undermine him at every turn anyway? Grey's irritability rose further.

Sophia fiddled with a button on her blouse—the one right at the centre of her breasts. 'I just put your laptop into the office for you—'

'Don't bother with the innocent act.' And she was driving him insane with that button.

To shore up his defences he said harshly and with abandoned licence, 'Your face is an open book. I can see everything you're thinking at any given moment.'

Her eyes widened and her gaze darted about the room in a trapped and guilty fashion. 'Can you really? My sisters bemoan the fact that I sometimes blurt exactly what's on my mind, but they haven't said anything about expressions on my face.' She glanced once towards the laundry room door, as though she'd like to run through it and keep running. 'Well, I'm sorry if you were annoyed that I took your laptop away.' She seemed to deliberately pull herself back to matters at hand. 'I realise you're frustrated at present but surely you could tell you needed rest by then? You've got injuries, medical conditions that will suffer if you push yourself too hard.'

Yes, he had pushed himself hard yesterday, had paid for it in the pain in his ankle and other general feelings of weariness, but how could he avoid that with a company to run? Now Grey wanted to defend his choices again, instead of focusing on her behaviour. How did she do that to him?

'If I'd really pushed over the line last night you'd have yelled for your laptop back before I got halfway down the stairs.' Her confidence said more about her understanding of his limits of tolerance than he had given her credit for.

He also noted the absence of any assurance that she wouldn't apply similar tactics in the future. Annoying woman. Insightful, too.

His gaze roved over the still crimson-streaked hair, lingering on the ponytail tied with a matching crimson ribbon. A jet-black figure-hugging blouse, cream trousers and yesterday's crimson boots covered her from head to foot... Was that cat fur on her blouse, just a few little strands of white?

'Domestic to the core,' he muttered in a tone that somehow changed from his intended gruffness to almost admiration. With a snort, Grey hobbled forward to sink into a chair at the table. She probably had a dozen cats in her apartment in Melbourne, making her home look cosy and welcoming. Rather, shedding hair all over the place. A non-domestic-seeking man's nightmare!

Maybe he needed food, fuel for his brain so he could think more clearly.

'I'm sorry. I didn't quite hear what you said.' She

took a saucepan off the stove and spooned its contents into two bowls. On the bench, the coffee percolator belched out a scent that wasn't quite ordinary.

'It was nothing.' Grey poured water into his glass and didn't feel any anticipation about the food whatsoever. He ate to keep up his strength and she was all he had in the way of someone to conveniently provide meals while he focused on other things. She could dish up the blandest most ordinary foods and he would feel no differently.

He'd been off on a flight of some kind of weird, incapacity-induced fancy when he'd thought he anticipated her next meal. Now he had his thoughts under control. He'd reprimanded Sophia, achieved what he'd set out to do.

He'd killed the attraction stone-dead as effectively, hadn't he, a sarcastic voice in his head put in.

Grey suppressed a second snort and grumbled, 'What's for breakfast? I'm hungry. It's making my head explode. And I brought the brace for you to put on. You seem to feel I shouldn't do it myself.'

'No, and I'm sure you want to do everything possible to get better.' She knelt at his feet and laced him up. Her movements were brisk and impersonal while those big sherry-coloured eyes fixed with way too much focus on first his foot and then his chin, his neck, even his ear.

Anything to avoid looking into his eyes, it seemed.

'Just one more tug to make sure it's snug enough.' She suited actions to words.

In a moment she would get up, move away from him. Then he wouldn't be able to smell her soft scent, touch the head bent to conceal her expression…

Grey's hand disengaged itself from his brain function. There could be no other explanation for the fact that he reached out to touch the silken hair on that down-bent head. A feather-light touch she wouldn't feel, wouldn't know about.

Yet he felt that touch and reacted to it in a way he couldn't explain. She had beautiful soft hair and a heart as big as Australia that drove her to send him demented with whatever manage-her-employer plan she had tucked away in that smart and sassy head of hers.

Inexplicably, a knot of something that felt like tenderness filled his chest. Grey yanked his hand back and leaned away from her.

'How does that feel?' She raised her gaze as she asked the question.

'The brace is as comfortable as it will get.' And her eyes were pools of liquid brown, her mouth soft and temptingly kissable.

She smiled that sunny smile even as she backed away from him and busied herself at the kitchen bench.

'Uh, here's breakfast.' Sophia carried the bowls

to the table and avoided looking into his eyes. She placed his bowl in front of him, pushed another of sliced bananas in some sort of brown, sticky sauce his way and returned to the bench to pour mugs of whatever she had brewed in the coffee percolator.

'The cereal is five grain porridge, slow cooked for forty minutes on the stove—triticale, oats, barley, wheat and rye.' She ticked the ingredients off on her fingers. 'I've percolated my own blend of morning coffee. It's decaf, but the cardamom flavour is so good you won't notice the absence of a caffeine kick.'

'I usually have toast or one of those snack breakfast bars you can buy off the shelf pre-wrapped and ready to go.' He always had coffee with breakfast—*real coffee*—and, yes, his doctor had said he should give it up completely, but surely fewer cups a day would do? 'I'm not really into coffee substitutes in the morning.'

But she'd already poured two big mugs of the brew. She put his on the table and paused to take the first sip of hers. The look that crossed her face as she absorbed the taste made his muscles clench.

Grey looked away. He had enough to cope with simply trying to control her and not desire her.

'I'll have the drink later, at my desk.' It wasn't capitulation. He would insist on some real coffee later this morning.

With a nod, Grey spooned banana goop on to the grain porridge, and dug in to start his meal.

They ate in silence. The porridge was chewy, filling, the caramelised bananas a nice touch on top.

'I'll start some work while you clean up and do whatever food preparation you need time for at this stage.' Mug of aromatic liquid in hand, he rose from the table and prepared to make a hasty exit—not running, just eager to start his working day.

Sophia stood and gestured towards his foot. 'Give me ten minutes and I'll be ready to help with the physio. I've brought oil from my room. It's not specifically for massage. I had it in my kit and it's just nice on your skin, but it will be great for your muscles. It must be difficult when you have to hobble all the time.'

'There's no need for oils or massage.' Grey closed his eyes and breathed deeply through his nose. All that achieved was to carry the scent of exotic spices from the mug in his hand and of Sophia—subtly perfumed and too close for comfort—to his senses.

No need for her to have her hands all over his bare skin either, even if only his leg.

'Oh, well, if you're sure.' She seemed disappointed.

He steeled himself against the thought, lest he begin to imagine just *why* she might feel that way. It was all to do with trying to look after him. Nothing else!

'I have to start work.' The bear growled the words in Grey's rumbly, aggravated voice. Long fingers clutched his mug like a lifeline and he moved to the office.

Grey seated himself at his desk and sipped his *not-coffee*, giving a soft sigh as the taste exploded on his tongue.

He propped his ankle on the cushion Sophia had provided yesterday and started to speak clearly and without growling into the voice recognition program.

He'd sorted everything out. He was in charge here.

Totally and completely in charge!

CHAPTER FOUR

SOPH cleaned up the kitchen, made early preparations for their lunch, tidied Grey's bathroom and bedroom and didn't pause once to breathe in his scent or think about him asleep with his head on the pillows as she plumped them and tossed them back on the bed.

'That tape first, please,' Grey said the moment she stepped into the office. He flicked a finger towards a tape on her desk but didn't lift his gaze from his computer screen. The voice recognition headphones were clamped on his head and he seemed content to ignore her.

'When will we break for your physio?' She could compromise about a time, but she didn't intend to skip the duty altogether.

'Ten o'clock. You can have more of your not-coffee drink ready for then.' He stopped with a frown. 'You'll probably want more of it and you might as well make the same for both of us. It will save time.'

Her lips twitched. 'Of course. That's very considerate of you.' He had liked the coffee. Why else would he want more?

'I'll give up about the massage for now,' she conceded, 'but I'm holding you to the physio, *and* half an hour outside in the sunshine, and a nap straight after lunch.' She bounced once—just slightly—on her seat as she sat down.

Then she turned to glare at him in the sternest imitation of one of his expressions she could manage. 'You'll just have to figure out what bits of work you can skip to make that all fit in.'

He cast a disgruntled look her way. 'And how do you propose I do that?'

'For starters you could give up reading and commenting on the detailed department reports that could be summed up in a line from the department head that says "Everything is fine" and replied to with one word from you. "Good".' Soph made this pronouncement and snapped her transcription headphones into place.

She then set about ignoring any response Grey might have made once he got over staring at her in disgusted fulminating shock.

The man appeared to have good personnel at work on his behalf, yet he made them report to him to the nth degree about every little thing.

In short, it appeared he was a control freak. She, on the other hand, would never be like that. She didn't push her own opinion or inveigle people into doing what she wanted. Nor did she suffer from an overweening urge to be helpful.

She was off topic, anyway. This was about Grey Barlow and…and his pushy opinions and behaviour.

Yes, that was what it was about.

Grey muttered something.

Soph didn't catch it.

He sighed and spoke more loudly. 'After you've done that tape, I'd like you to get on to the Internet, please, and research…' He rattled off the information he wanted, made sure she'd jotted it all down and turned back to his work.

Setting aside her questions for now, Soph did what he had asked.

For the rest of the morning her employer focused almost exclusively on the deal that was in trouble—and it clearly *was* in trouble.

The longer he worked, the more guilt gnawed at her. 'Did my re-routing the phone yesterday lunch time contribute to these problems?' she blurted when he had a break in phone calls.

His gaze snapped to hers. For a moment he stared at her blankly, and then he shook his head. 'The Beacon's Cove project has been difficult from the start, unfortunately.' His expression softened. 'You didn't create any added difficulties, and I know you meant well.'

At this niceness, a fresh burst of honesty forced its way out of her. She had to do something to combat the mushy up-swell of happiness. 'Sometimes I do things simply because I decide they're right, without maybe consulting much beforehand—'

'No kidding?' His mockery was gentle.

He went back to work.

Soph relaxed—sort of—as much as she could when in the same room as Grey, and a less snarly Grey, at that. Would it last? What if it did and she liked him that way as much as she liked the grumpy version?

'You can be a little overbearing, yourself.' But the tension had drained out of her so that she smiled as she said it, and then got back to work.

'Will you get those two sheets off the printer and fax them for me?' Grey asked some time later and moved his foot on the cushion beneath his desk.

With a nod, Soph walked to the other side of the room. As she sent the fax, the phone rang again.

'Barlow.' Grey took the call himself.

Soph assumed it would be more about the Beacon's Cove project and listened with half an ear.

'You have a generous stipend, Leanna. I've explained what you need to do to manage it.' He sounded both tolerant and frustrated, and his face looked kind of empty, maybe even a little sad.

That last made Soph start across the room towards him, though she didn't know what she would do when she got there. She stopped again when he went on.

'If you're in trouble, sell off some of the goods you bought that maxed out your cards and use the money to pay off your debts.'

A short pause ensued in which Soph hovered and shuffled the papers in her hands, not quite knowing whether to go to her desk and pretend she wasn't listening or leave the room to give him privacy.

He spoke again. 'Now that's sorted, I guess I'll speak with you some time and…thanks for asking after my health. Goodbye, Leanna.' He ended the call and rubbed the back of his neck.

Well, there didn't seem much point in ignoring what had happened. 'I take it one of your past stepmothers likes spending money?'

'They all do.' He spoke with weariness, not rancour. 'My father encouraged the trait during his time with each of them and, to his credit, he set them all up generously and equally when the relationships ended and left them well provided for at his death. They just don't always manage their money very well.'

'I can't imagine having three different mothers.' Soph hadn't got much joy out of her sole experience. 'My sisters and I only had the one. She wasn't exactly maternal at any time, and she left altogether with my father when I was still in early high school.'

'It was four wives my father had, actually.' He gave

an uncomfortable shrug of his shoulders. 'My mother died when I was five years old. I don't remember much about her. I've forgotten a lot of it, actually. Domesticity really isn't my thing.' He paused and drew a breath. 'I'm sorry about your past…'

He was, she could tell. But he was also warning her off.

'I'm sorry about yours. Anyway, my situation is no biggie.' She waved the sympathy away even as she accepted the sting of his words.

Domesticity really isn't my thing.

He had simply confirmed what she'd suspected. Perhaps the words saddened her because they made for a lonely future for him? Yes, it must be that.

And what about your future, Soph? When will you *be ready to trust in love?*

A silly thought. She could be ready any time, if she chose to be.

'My sisters were all I needed, anyway.' She focused on that and pushed the other thoughts aside.

Grey probably preferred not to think about all this. For his sake she needed to come up with a change of subject now. It was a forte of hers to take the heat off, so why could she only gaze at him, at the wounded arm in its cast with another loose pullover top pushed up above his elbow like yesterday? At the width of shoulders she had seen unclothed even though she'd been uninvited at the time?

Why couldn't she forget how he looked, how she reacted to him? 'Um…'

'In regard to the Beacon's Cove project—all the faxes and phone calls this morning have taken the matter as far as it can go without some stronger discussion.' Grey found the change of topic for her.

Soph leaped on it with relief. 'What can I do to help?'

'I want you to set up a visual link on the computer. I've sent emails to schedule a meeting for—' he glanced at the clock on the wall '—fifteen minutes from now. I'll hear feedback from the other departments first, and then discuss Beacon's Cove with my two most senior department heads.'

He outlined how the visual link worked and what she needed to do to set it up. 'I'll go upstairs and change clothes. I prefer to greet my senior staff in a suit, even if it will be *sans* jacket this time.'

Matching actions to words, he rose from his desk and moved through the doorway. Soph stood there and couldn't seem to shift her feet until she realised the minutes were ticking away.

It was possible that she may not have exactly taken in every little nuance of how to set up the link for the conference. She grabbed the pile of cords and plugs he had said she should use and started to unravel them.

After grappling with various bits and ends for

several minutes, Soph had to admit defeat. She picked up the phone and called her brother-in-law on his private line at his Melbourne shipping office.

'Nate Barrett.' Just the calm tone helped her take a deep breath.

'It's me, Soph. Do you know how to set up a visual conference thingy on the computer?' She explained what she had done, all Grey's directions and the resulting non-event currently on the screen.

Her brother-in-law chuckled and sorted her out in about thirty seconds, then asked about her new job, when the family might expect to see her, and shared his daughter's latest exploits.

These included squealing in her great-grandfather's ear, getting into everything at ground level and being able to make 'phhtpht' noises—a raspberry without the bubbles—this she usually demonstrated in a silent moment in the queue at the bank or the grocers.

'She's the cleverest nine-month-old in existence,' her father boasted.

'Naturally.' Soph laughed, then heard steps approach behind her. 'Gotta go, Nate. I love you so much for helping me. Bye.'

'A personal call?' Grey asked in a carefully neutral tone, but the look in his eyes wasn't neutral. It was snappish. And interested. In a way he clearly didn't want to be.

'Not really a personal call, no.' In a tone a little too breathless for her comfort, she went on to explain. 'I phoned my brother-in-law and asked him to help me figure out the problem with your conference link. I didn't want to disturb you while you were dressing and there wasn't a lot of spare time.'

'You got it sorted?' His gaze remained locked on her.

'Yes, I think I have it under control.' She wasn't sure about herself, though. Because she took a proper look at him then—not only into his eyes—and her heart climbed up and lodged in her throat at the sight he made.

'Ah, you look, ah—' Stunning, gorgeous, overwhelmingly male and powerful and compelling. All those words fitted. Soph settled for a lame, '—businesslike.'

He moved forward and she saw the faint tinge of heat high on his cheekbones. Because she had complimented him? Or maybe because he'd read all the things she didn't say when their gazes had met? Oh, she didn't want him to think she was fixated on him!

'A suit,' she said quickly, her aplomb gone, 'suits you.'

At that he smiled, and her heart flipped over again.

'I need your help.' His smile faded into something a whole lot less cheerful.

The disgruntled expression deepened as he went

on to explain what he needed. 'The top buttonhole is tight. I can't do it up one-handed and I can't do the tie at all.'

'No problem.' She wouldn't allow there to be any problems. This was just business, even if it was the first time he'd admitted he actually needed her help, and that admission made her all warm and happy, which was a really, really foolish reaction on her part, and she would have to get up close and personal with his body…

'It's just buttons and a tie,' she muttered, took the tie from his hand and tossed it on to the desk. 'I'll do the button first. Sorry if I strangle you a bit in the process. It's not as easy when you're not the one wearing the shirt.'

'Have a lot of experience with other people's buttons, do you?' The words were low and instantly regretted if the look on his face was any indication.

Yeah. Real smart to be pleased that he was still fighting an attraction to her. The point was he *did* fight it. He *didn't want* to feel that way. Same as she didn't.

Grey was still looking at her and, despite his annoyance, he couldn't seem to draw his gaze away.

Soph resorted to ignoring the problem and did the button up as fast as she could. She reached for the tie and put it around her own neck where she could lower her gaze and focus on making a loose knot.

'I dressed the occasional doll during my childhood.' She kept a deliberate light tone in her voice but her senses remained heightened in awareness of him.

She transferred the tie to his neck, fixed it just so and tilted her head to examine the results. 'You look fine.' Too fine for her peace of mind, but she couldn't seem to help that at the moment.

'I'd be happier in the jacket as well, but at least I managed to get the shirt over the cast.' The cuff of that sleeve hung open. 'Thank you for helping me to look as respectable as I can.'

He did that. Grumped his head off, and then let her know he noted and appreciated her efforts, even if just in a hint about not-coffee. The man had his contradictions. It was a pity Soph found those contradictions intriguing rather than irritating or just plain unappealing.

'I'm glad I could help, and I'm sure you'll put out a good image to your staff.'

He stepped around her, moved to his desk, sat and positioned his foot on the cushion.

It was a reprieve, a chance for her to pull herself together. Soph sat, laid her hands on the computer keyboard and hoped she could type a coherent sentence.

The man had simply appeared in business clothing. It was *no big deal.*

'It's time for the conference. Type your notes straight into the computer and save the data often.'

He spoke without looking at her. 'Don't worry about making it neat. Just get the details down.'

Grey gave Sophia her instructions and turned his attention to his visual conference. What the hell was wrong with him, anyway? Maybe the blood pressure prescription the doctor had forced on him had messed with his mind. There had to be some explanation for his ongoing, deepening and completely unwelcome response to his temporary assistant.

'It's quite ridiculous,' he muttered, then snapped to attention when he realised his mind had wandered. 'Sorry, Jones. Please repeat what you just said. The link went fuzzy for a moment.' The link inside Grey's head, that was.

After reports from the others, Grey dismissed them, and Coates and McCarty filled him in on the Beacon's Cove project. They admitted the news wasn't good.

'Tell me what you know—' Grey leaned forward in his chair '—and everything you're thinking. There has to be a way for us to resolve this so we don't end up losing those millions.'

A small gasp came from Sophia before her fingers continued on her keyboard with renewed vigour. Grey took no notice. He didn't notice anything, in truth, until he ended the conference two hours later and realised he wasn't exactly relaxed. He rubbed at his breastbone. Something in there felt tied in knots.

'I've saved all the notes on to the computer. Do you want me to try to correlate them, put them into point form or something before I get dinner? I've had no chance to start a meal.' Soph asked it tentatively because, well, she didn't deal in millions of dollars and the idea of her employer possibly *losing* such an amount of money on a single deal gone wrong boggled her mind.

Grey turned his glance her way and seemed almost surprised to see her still seated there. There were lines of strain around his mouth. 'I think at this stage you can just keep the notes and we'll refer to them if I want to check on details about anything that was said. Maybe you could organise something quick for us to eat.' Frustration leached through his weariness and into his words. 'Then—I don't know. I'm limited in what I can do from here. I've told the others to do what they can…' He trailed off.

Soph prepared coconut-topped apricot egg custard and put it in the oven to bake. While it cooked she whipped together a vegetable stir-fry and savoury glazed meatballs in a mango chutney sauce. She got the food on the table quickly and, when she heard no signs of movement close by, went searching for Grey.

She found him reclined on the sofa in the living room, his foot up, the physio sheet on the coffee table in front of him. His eyes were closed, his skin pale beneath his tan. The man was exhausted, but not asleep. He looked up as he heard her approach.

'You look ill.' She watched his gaze slowly focus on her and hoped he wouldn't choose to growl. Not while he looked like this.

'I'm fine. There's no pain. A little discomfort in the ankle, but that's nothing new and the rest has settled.' He got to his feet, swaying slightly before he found his balance.

What rest? Soph wanted to rush forward and prop him up but she could imagine how well that would be received. 'Come and eat, then. Maybe the energy boost will help. The food isn't overly spiced.' She thought of him rubbing his chest. 'If you have indigestion…'

'There is nothing wrong with my digestion.' He cut her a monster-snarl look from beneath beetled brows. 'Do we have to discuss this?'

'No, I guess not.' Did he think indigestion was unmanly or something? Soph let him eat in peace after that and was pleased to see the colour come back into his face, but he *had* looked quite wan for a while there.

Even so, when the meal finally ended and Grey sat back with a satisfied sound, she knew she had to at least let him catch up on the rest of his news.

'I have phone messages from when you were busy with other matters this afternoon.' His concentration had been absorbed while he'd worked on the Beacon's Cove project, so she wasn't sure if he had listened in on any of those calls. 'There's nothing urgent, but you'll want to be informed.'

'Perhaps we could do the physio stretches while you fill me in.' He got to his feet as he made the suggestion and headed for the living room.

Soph, perforce, followed and started the exercise routine as she recited the details of several calls from business people who had asked that Grey contact them.

Grey nodded. 'You're right; there's nothing urgent there. I'll return the calls over the next couple of days.'

'That only leaves three more.' His stepmothers were persistent, if nothing else. Soph finished the exercises and sat back beside him on the two-seater sofa. 'All your stepmothers phoned again today. Dawn and Sharon wanted your response on their urgent requests…for um…a cruise and a charter plane, and Leanna thought you should re-examine the size of their stipends. She said something about inflation. They all asked after your health again, as well.'

'I'll phone them…some time soon. Not tonight. I plan to have a long soak in the tub and turn in.' He sighed and pushed up on to his feet. 'I suppose you'll insist I have sleep aids again.'

He sounded very long-suffering as he said this, but Soph knew—he really wanted the incense and tea.

They had obviously helped, even if he was too proud to say so. *And* he was choosing to get more rest.

Would wonders never cease? 'I'll be happy to bring more incense and chamomile tea.'

'Thank you.' He turned and started towards the staircase. 'I have appointments with my GP and a physiotherapist in Melbourne tomorrow. The first appointment is at ten-thirty. We'll stay the night at my town house. You should have an early night as well so you're fresh to do the driving.'

'Oh, well, a trip to Melbourne will be nice.' He really wasn't the sort who blabbed out all his plans way in advance, was he? Soph could have done with some time to mentally prepare herself for a long car trip in his company. She tried to look on the bright side. 'We can get to know each other better during the drive. For now, I'll come up and run your bath.'

'I'll take care of the bath myself. If you'll leave the incense and tea in my room, we needn't see each other again until morning.' He turned away as though he had already forgotten her existence.

'I'll put the tea in an insulated mug for you so it stays warm.' Soph kept pace with him as he moved towards the staircase. 'I can come in to see the doctor and physiotherapist with you tomorrow, if you like. Some people are squeamish about visiting medical people—'

'I can manage my own appointments.' He gritted

the words through his teeth as he paused at the base of the stairs. The glance he cast her way threatened strangulation by remote glare if she said another word on the topic of assisting him.

Soph suppressed the hint of a grin that wanted to escape.

'Just see to it you're ready to go in time in the morning. I don't want any complications or last-minute problems.'

It was then that Soph remembered there *was* a complication. He was outside, probably chomping grass and food pellets. How could she have overlooked the implications of an overnight trip?

'There won't be any problems.' Guilty heat climbed her neck and settled in her cheeks. 'Why would you think there might be?'

She just had to work out how to make the Alfie situation *not* be a problem. Soph waved a hand towards the staircase. 'Er, well, goodnight. I'll bring the tea and incense while you're bathing. I'll be in and out of your room in less than ten seconds.'

Though he cast her a frown, he dipped his head in acknowledgement and wrapped his hand around the balustrade. 'Goodnight.'

'Yes. Goodnight. Sweet dreams.' Soph nodded. 'I'll see you in the morning, when I'm sure everything will be totally uncomplicated and calm and relaxed.'

'Right.' He gave her an odd look and disappeared up the staircase.

Soph stood at the bottom and chewed her lip. She couldn't leave Alfie here alone for that long.

Some time between now and morning, she had to figure out what to do about a certain rescued pet!

CHAPTER FIVE

AT QUARTER to seven the next morning, Soph sat in her bed cuddling Alfred the smuggled rabbit. No great revelation had come to her in the middle of the night and she was somewhat…worried. 'We just have to tell him, Alfie, because I cannot and will not leave you alone here for that amount of time.'

She swung her legs over the side of the bed, aware that she should have said something to Grey before now instead of sneaking the rabbit in at night, but the moment had just never been right and then he'd made his sudden announcement that they were to stay overnight in Melbourne.

He wasn't keen on domesticity. Okay, he seemed to feel it was right up there with having teeth pulled, maybe worse. How could she subject Alfie to such negativity?

Downstairs, the phone began to ring. Soph popped Alfie into his high basket and tugged her door across after her. It didn't catch, but that wouldn't matter. She hurried downstairs and snatched up the phone, remembering to give the usual businesslike greeting, despite the early hour. 'Sophia Gable on behalf of Mr Grey Barlow; how may I help you?'

A man apologised for phoning so early and asked if Grey was up and about yet. 'I'm Charles Cooper, Grey's doctor.'

Soph's hand tightened a little around the phone. 'I can get him for you. Is it urgent? Is there a problem?' She thought to add, 'I'm Mr Barlow's temporary assistant while he's recovering from his injuries.'

'Hmph. Perhaps the boy has some sense, after all.' Dr Cooper cleared his throat in a noisy, blustery way. 'No need to disturb him. I phoned to make sure he will be at his appointment today.'

'He'll be there. We've already made our plans.' Most of them, except the bit where she explained the need to take a rabbit with them.

'Good to hear.' The doctor paused. 'What do you think about his stress levels? Do you see any indication of improvement in that regard?'

'Stress levels.' Soph repeated the words while something hard lodged in the pit of her stomach. 'I wasn't aware of those.' But it made sense. The pale face yesterday, Grey rubbing at his breastbone while she'd thought he had indigestion or heartburn…

'Grey has history on both sides of the family that

indicate he needs to take care and, right now, his blood pressure is up, along with several other issues that seem to suggest he's pushing himself.' The doctor said a few blistering words about Grey's hard-headedness. 'I delivered the lad, you know, and he's been stubborn from day one.'

'I can imagine that.' Soph kept her tone mild, though she suspected *her* blood pressure might be climbing right now!

'You said you're his assistant.' The doctor's voice rose in question. 'Don't tell me he's been working from there?'

'Yes, he's worked quite long days. Keeping track of his company takes all of his time.' Long days that could only have harmed him. 'I tried to slow him down—'

'The stay in the country was to ensure he had a complete break from contact with work.' Again, the doctor harrumphed. 'I've talked to him about this.'

'I see.' And Soph did. She saw herself working like crazy to help her employer push himself into the ground, when apparently he had health issues he hadn't considered worth a mention. Even when she had made it clear that she needed to look after him in the right way.

By his silence, he had actively *stopped her* from helping him.

'My employer will be at your appointment,

doctor.' Did the words sound on the irritable side? Well, then, they matched Soph's current mood. 'I hope you'll ask him how much time he's invested in rest and recuperation. It could prove an interesting discussion for you.'

Soph finished the phone call with the lovely, good, sensible doctor. It wasn't his fault that her employer chose to dice with his well-being. She stomped up the staircase and fumed over the fact that she had worked her fingers to the bone since she'd got here, all to help Grey probably raise his stress levels even further than they had been. *That* was something worthy of her feelings.

'Good morning. Did I hear the phone?' The low rumbled words came from Grey's opened doorway.

She looked up and came to a halt. Bare skin, rumpled hair, sleepy eyes that watched her with interest and made her suddenly aware that she wore only a green spaghetti strap top and long floral pyjama pants with her hair a riot of unstyled mess about her face.

Soph returned his examination. Looked at the expanse of his chest, the light dusting of hair, the overall appearance of a man who had just climbed out of bed. Even his feet looked appealing. Soph had never cared less about feet. She didn't now. She was angry—nothing else!

'You shouldn't walk without the exoform support

on your foot.' She regained her stomp factor and used it to move towards him. 'Where is it? I'll put it on for you.'

'The brace is in my room.' He leaned behind him and used his good hand to push the door wide, but didn't take his gaze from her. 'You haven't explained about the phone call.'

It was irritation that made her blood heat, nothing else, certainly not being close to him, no matter what her early morning hormone levels might want to say to her.

She didn't care if Grey had just climbed out of that bed, either. No, sir. Soph did not care. She pushed past him, into his room, snatched up the brace and pointed to the rumpled bed. 'Sit.'

Only when he did and she had deftly and carefully laced and tied the brace without once thinking about the proximity of all that bare skin—*not once*—did Soph look up and meet his gaze again.

He narrowed his eyes. 'Why are you angry?'

Oh, she was annoyed, all right, along with other feelings she couldn't begin to sort out right now. She stuck to the anger part and let him have it.

'The call,' she informed him with slow conciseness, biting each word off before she spoke the next, 'was from your doctor. He rang to check you'd be at your appointment today. I said you would be.'

As she talked, she stepped away until she stood

in the corridor, but only because if she stayed close to Grey right now she might pummel him.

'What else did he say?' Grey followed her, stalking after her. How could he seem to stalk when in truth he had no choice but to hobble? It was that blasted presence of his. Grey went on, 'I can see in your face there was more.'

'You've deliberately misled me.' The accusation came straight out of her anxiety and anger. 'I came here to care for you and help you get well and instead you used me to help you work like a madman.'

Unable to stop herself, she moved towards him. 'The doctor told you to get right away from your workload, didn't he? Yet you've done the exact opposite and hauled it all here with you.'

Why didn't you trust me with your problems? All of them? Why wasn't I good enough for that?

'I have responsibilities.' The muscles around Grey's mouth tightened and his lips thinned. He took a step forward until they were almost nose to nose. 'I've built that company up into what it is today. *I* have. I've every right to watch over it, and Doc Cooper had no business discussing my health with you that way.'

'I suppose that's true. I'm just the person hired to help you and care for you for the next few weeks.' She jutted her chin at him and, no, she did not see any parallels between his absurd attitude and her own need to control any and all emotional entanglements.

This was about his behaviour. 'Why didn't you tell me? I could have done so much more. The doctor said you have concerns in your family history that mean you have to be extra careful.'

'My mother died young of a heart attack. My father followed five years ago from problems caused by living the high life for too long. But *I'm* not sick. Not in the way the doctor is worried about.'

Frustration poured off him. 'I've been nothing but healthy. The doctor is overreacting to a few readings he got soon after my accident that could have resulted from the shock of breaking my arm, the pain, anything.'

Soph stared at the stubborn man and tried to hold on to her anger, but something stronger supplanted it. He didn't say much about his father, didn't seem close to his stepmothers, and couldn't remember much of his mother. How much of his life had he spent feeling detached and maybe alone?

Yes, she felt sad for him but she still felt hurt.

Well, from now on she would tend to him in a very businesslike manner. Forget letting herself actually *care*.

'Look, I know I've annoyed you.' He rammed his hand through his hair, ruffling it into further disarray as he seemed to search for words. 'I'm sorry I wasn't more open. I'm not accustomed to being helped.'

Now he looked wickedly tempting and sorry as

well as infuriating and upsetting and still… isolated somehow.

'So you'll let me help you properly from now on?' she mumbled.

'If you still want to, I'll try.' He spoke the words in a low, soft tone that felt like the stroke of a hand. Or, at the least, of a bear's paw without the claws.

Soph sighed as the remaining shreds of her anger dissipated. 'I still want to.'

Silence fell then and she slowly became aware of other things. The quiet huff of his breath in the stillness, the warm heat of his body…

Her eyes widened and she looked up and gasped, because somehow the distance between them had all but disappeared as they'd had it out about his health issues. Now Grey watched her, his face tight as his gaze darkened and swept over her, caught her up with the strength of a physical touch.

'This isn't working, is it?' His hand rose to clasp her arm.

Just that simple touch shifted all through her. Soph's hand followed the lead of his and pressed against the wall of his chest. He growled, but this time it wasn't Bear Speak.

Her heart rate doubled and her breath caught in her throat as she realized, *He's going to kiss me*.

She could have backed away, said or done something to stop him, but she didn't. She waited. And then his lips were warm and sure over hers, determined and seeking and demanding all at once, and Soph kissed him back while sensations bombarded her.

The satin of his lips against hers, the taste and texture of him and the low sound of satisfaction he made as their heads angled and the kiss deepened. His heart beat steady and sure beneath her fingertips. Warm skin and the masculine feel of crisp, curly hair burned against the pads of her fingers.

His hand released her arm and rose to cup her face while his other arm wrapped around her back and drew her in, against his body. He didn't seem to care that both his upper arm and the plaster cast were pressed to her.

They kissed like that, body to body, soft full lips to firm silky ones, for long head-spinning moments until finally they drew apart just enough to breathe in, for their gazes to meet.

The barrier of flimsy clothes between them felt like nothing. They could have been in polar suits on an iceberg and she still would have felt his heat and responded with her own. The strength of that reaction to him scared her, because she had kissed men but it had never been like this.

Yet she had let it happen, had fully participated.

Because you were curious, because ignoring it wasn't working.

Sure, and this had worked better?

'I don't know—' What to do, how to react, how to respond to this intensity.

'Neither do I.' He pulled back and stepped away from her.

'That was…um…it was unexpected.' The heat, how quickly it had moved from curiosity to a demand that had all but swept her away. Had it affected him equally or did he see it as just another kiss, no big deal?

'Unexpected, and not smart.' His voice was gravelly, his face tight and leashed in a way that made her heart pound all over again.

This *had* affected him. That conclusion made her feel powerful and pleased with herself when she shouldn't.

'No, it wasn't smart.' She had to agree. When her body caught up with her thought processes she would mean every word.

'I usually have better control. I *always* have control.' He clamped his lips closed.

He would have that control again. Soph didn't doubt it. Even now he was gathering himself, drawing his strength around him. He would use it to shut her out because he *wanted* to control himself far, far away from any interest in her.

'I understand you probably wish that hadn't happened, but I think it had to because we were both curious.' She tipped up her chin, cool on the outside. 'Now we've put that curiosity to rest. It won't be repeated and we can get on with the working relationship we want.'

'Yes.' His eyes narrowed. 'That's exactly how I see it.'

'I'd like to discuss our working relationship now, actually.' Soph forced her thoughts in that direction by sheer effort of will. 'I have some stipulations. Just so I'm sure we're both clear.'

'If you're worried about this…' His brows drew together. 'What are the stipulations?'

Not those. She knew he didn't want this to happen again. 'You agree to be honest with me about your health from now on and you take real steps to do what your doctor has asked of you.' She *needed* that agreement from him—to satisfy her commitment to her work for him. If there were other reasons, she would sort them out.

Unsettled, she pushed on, determined to at least convince Grey that their kiss hadn't completely crumbled every rational thought from her mind. 'I need to know you'll let me do my job here.'

His gaze softened. 'I will let you do your job.'

'Thank you. It's better to be completely open.' They had openly kissed, had agreed not to repeat the experience. He had agreed to let her help him properly.

'So you'd say honesty and openness are important between us?' His glance moved to a point beyond her left shoulder and his eyebrows rose into twin questioning arcs.

Soph dipped her head and wondered why she felt a little unnerved by his expression. 'Yes. Those things are important.'

'Then don't you think it's odd,' he said, 'that the house has suddenly sprouted a giant white rat? A rat who seems rather attached to you? Who just emerged from your room?'

'A giant white rat,' she repeated stupidly, but she knew. Oh, she knew. With a sense of the inevitable, Soph turned her head and, sure enough, there was Alfie. Not a giant rat, no, and her employer knew this. But Alfie was a glaring example that she hadn't given the full disclosure she had just ranted about, and so the word 'rat' did hold a certain metaphoric impact.

Alfie twitched his nose and came forward, flop ears flopping, to sit at her feet in a fluffy, incriminating bundle.

Blast.

In fact, double drat darn blast with a triple pike and a twist. She glanced up, about to beg, convinced that Grey would be glaring in appalled revulsion.

Domesticity really isn't my thing.

Did his mouth twitch before he firmed it? Or had she hallucinated that idea when in fact he truly was angry?

'You're very righteous about me keeping things

from you, Sophia,' he drawled, 'but clearly you've done the same.'

'I confess.' There didn't seem to be any other option. Maybe if she just confronted it, it wouldn't be *too* awful? 'I smuggled a rabbit into the house. I've smuggled him in at night since I got here, but I had every intention of telling you about him. This morning, in fact.'

Soph scooped Alfie up and held him against her chest. The feel of his soft fur soothed her frazzled edges, just a little.

Just enough for her to feel the full strength of her embarrassment.

'My reasons were different.' Guilty heat swept into her face. Well, now that her secret was out, she might as well get the rest over with.

'Alfred has to come with us to Melbourne. We'll need to leave in time to settle him in the yard at your town house before we go to your first appointment.'

'Is he car and house trained?' Grey eyed the rabbit dubiously.

Soph drew a deep breath. 'He hasn't had an accident yet.'

Grey lifted an eyebrow. 'And how long is "yet"?'

'Um, one day longer than I've been here. Well, just a night longer, actually.' Soph turned away so she wouldn't have to meet his gaze. 'I found him abandoned near my flat the night before I came here.'

'And you adopted him.' He made it sound inevitable.

'Yes.' Why did she feel that Grey had just looked deep inside her and discovered a secret she should have guarded more carefully? What was he thinking? 'I adopted him.'

'Well, I guess I know what the strands of white fur were on your shirt, now.' He moved towards his room. 'Not cat fur, but still as domestic.'

She knew just how much Grey liked domestic. 'Um, so do you mind if he…uh…?'

'I'm turning over a new leaf, remember?' He paused in the doorway of his room and looked at her over his shoulder. 'I may not like the idea of a pet on board, but I agreed to get along.'

'I'll get ready, then.' She didn't know what else to say.

As Grey closed his door, Soph leaned against hers.

She felt as though she had just endured a battle. Not because of Alfie, but because of Grey and his secretiveness and their kiss and his surprising tolerance about her pet.

Soph was confused.

And she didn't know if the battle was over yet.

CHAPTER SIX

SOPH gave herself a stern talking-to during the drive from her employer's country home to his Melbourne town house. She had plenty of opportunity to do so as they sat in silence in the sleek, bullet-grey sedan. So much for the 'getting to know you better' conversation she had envisaged. Alfie sat in his basket in the back. He was very well-behaved.

The Melbourne skyline closed around them. Cars rushed along and people hurried about their business while a brisk wind pushed at their backs. Soph's thoughts moved at the same determined pace as she made her way to Grey's suburb.

She had got off track on this assignment—that was the trouble. Grey's kissing her hadn't helped. It had opened up thoughts and temptations she must ignore.

From now on she would be the sensible, controlled professional she should have portrayed from the start. Soph glanced at her French-braided uncoloured blonde hair in the rear-view mirror and gave an all but imperceptible nod.

'The next right is my street.' Grey gave the direction as he had all the others, with little inflection and no waste of words.

'Thanks.' She turned into yet another posh residential street.

'My town house is the one with the blue trim, just ahead.' Grey pointed out a perfectly gorgeous home nestled between two others that, despite also being gorgeous, did nothing for her at all even though they should have impressed her equally.

She was out of sorts! Thoughts about trusting others, memories about her parents leaving and odd nebulous aches and feelings towards her sisters had plagued her during the drive. As if all the tension with Grey hadn't been enough.

Anyway, his house was probably perfectly horrid inside, cold and sterile with ugly furnishings and inexplicable art that had cost megadollars on all the walls.

She clenched her teeth. 'Let me get Alfie settled so we can make our way to your first appointment.'

'The house has a security system. I'll need to disarm it for you.' Did he sound a little baffled? Frustrated with her or simply frustrated, full stop? Confused? Fed up? Still overly aware in ways he shouldn't be?

Actually, she was starting to list her own feelings.

Grey's gaze kept going to her hair and then over the rest of her—the white blouse with the lace ruffle on the front, the plain skirt and black pumps. She kind of wished she had on blue nail polish and a big chunky necklace, but she didn't and she felt *just fine, as powerful as she needed to be.*

'Sorry to have to bother you, then.' She got out of the car and hauled Alfie's fold-up enclosure from the boot. By then, Grey was out of the car and had Alfie in his basket tucked under his good arm.

He wanted to help? Be a wonderful, considerate gentleman despite his injuries? Pretend to tolerate the rabbit?

Soph didn't have to fall prey to any of this. She accompanied him to the front door, waited while he unlocked it and inputted his security code and followed him in. She didn't even notice the beautiful wainscoting or the huge potted ornamental orange tree or the lovely rich curtains and squishy furniture that made the place a quiet haven and anything but sterile or cold. Nope. She didn't notice any of it at all.

They didn't linger. When Soph drew the car to a halt in the car park behind the doctor's rooms some time later, Grey turned to her.

'This shouldn't take long. You can window shop or whatever you like and meet me at the coffee place next door in, say, half an hour. I can always wait for you if I get out sooner.'

It was the most he'd said to her in one go since this morning and an obvious dismissal. Yet he seemed edgy and, from the standpoint of ensuring that he kept her informed, Soph decided it wouldn't be appropriate to leave him. She wasn't *emotionally involved* in his care. This was just common sense stuff.

'I prefer to wait in the waiting room. That's the most efficient course of action.' They'd made an agreement. He might not like it but she expected him to stick to it.

'Fine.' He glared and turned his gaze away from hers. 'It's this way.'

He didn't have to wait long, which was probably just as well, and then Soph sat there…and sat. What could be taking them so long?

After fifty minutes Soph was a wreck, but only because she wanted to make a successful work experience out of her time with Grey. She wasn't worried sick and off on flights of imagination about his health issues, all of them doomsday-oriented.

When Grey finally emerged she leapt up from her seat and met him at the edge of the waiting room. 'Are you all right? What did the doctor say? You were gone so long I thought maybe he'd found something awful and rushed you out the back to a waiting ambulance…' She forced the words to a stop, realizing that she had her fingers wrapped around Grey's forearm in a crushing grip.

Touching him had sent a zing up her arm and into her chest too. They'd kissed, hadn't they, and nothing was the same now, no matter how hard she tried to believe otherwise.

Not the time to think about it! She released her hold on him.

Grey stared into her eyes with a rare uncertainty in his own. Memory of that stolen kiss flared in his gaze before he stepped away and his jaw tightened.

'Let me pay for the visit.' He moved to the front desk, tugged out his wallet and quickly took care of business.

The junior secretary gazed at him with flirtatious eyes. Grey thanked her politely and didn't appear to notice. As they left, he suggested they make their way to the physiotherapist's office area. 'We can have lunch at the sushi bar next door to it. I didn't expect to be as long as I was with Dr Cooper.'

No, and something told her he hadn't got the results he'd hoped for. Soph started worrying again. She held off saying anything more until they were in the bar and their meals had arrived and then the waiting got too much for her. 'Well? What's the verdict? Are you all better or heaps worse? You've been grim and silent since we left the doctor's rooms.'

'The readings hadn't gone down—not even the blood pressure, which should have responded to the medication at least a little by now.' He sounded disgusted and something else. Not chastised, exactly, but a bit shaken, perhaps? 'The doctor is convinced the problems were there already and having the accident simply got them noticed.'

She did her best to tread carefully as she asked, 'Does this mean genetic factors really could be an issue?'

'Dr Cooper is inclined to believe that some of this may be inherited. He's not expecting heart failure…'

Soph sensed a bit of a 'but' on the end of that. 'So he said he won't worry about your heart provided—?'

'Provided I take care of the other matters, and take care of myself overall.' He drew a deep breath. 'I have to fix the problem, now that I know it's more than a blip.'

He probably hated that he'd been wrong. His next words seemed to confirm that.

'I've always taken care of my health. I don't fill my body with crappy foods or drink to excess, and I keep fit.'

'Well, of course you do. A person only has to see your physique. It's all muscled. You haven't got an ounce of fat on you…' She shoved a bite-sized Maki-zushi into her mouth and glanced uneasily at the diners all around them. The sushi bar was packed, but nobody appeared to be listening to their conversation.

Except Grey himself, who cast one heightened glance at her before he locked it down and took a bite of his food.

'What will you do, Grey?' Their earlier antagonism and subsequent passion set aside for the moment, Soph wanted to help.

He smiled at her then—smiled with a curve of the lips that had kissed her with such hunger—and Soph suppressed a sigh because he really did appeal to her so much. How could her protestations hold up when he looked at her this way?

'You really do have a kind heart, don't you? This morning you were furious with me but you're willing to forgive and just move on.' He broke eye contact and for a few minutes they ate in silence. Finally he pushed his plate away.

'I can hold a grudge,' she said with a hint of offence as she crumpled her napkin on to her plate.

Grey glanced at the watch on his wrist. 'We should head for the physiotherapist's offices now, I think.' As he stood, his smile faded. 'I'll do what the doctor suggested in the first place. Complete rest for a few days. I may not like it and I'll probably go mad in the process, but I'll take the necessary steps to bring everything under control.'

'Ah, okay.' A few days? That would do it? Soph was dubious but she couldn't discuss it further. The physiotherapist's offices were right next door, and the receptionist sent Grey straight in for his appointment.

Soph cooled her heels again. When he emerged, they went to the car and he sat there and made a phone call to his office. 'I want a meeting with the head of every department. Get them to reshuffle their schedules to make it work. For any head not in Melbourne today have someone stand in.'

Grey finished the phone call and turned to her. 'We need to go straight to my company building now. After I've taken care of things there, we'll go back to the town house.' He paused and frowned.

For a moment frustration lurked, but he clamped his teeth shut over it and turned his head to look through the windscreen of the car.

Soph drove and when she finally pulled the car to a stop in his company's underground car park, she said quietly, 'You'll probably prefer me to wait here.' She'd never parked in a company director's space before and tried for some levity. 'I hope no one thinks I'm trying to steal your car.'

'No, I want you to come with me.' He looked at her then—really looked, his expression resigned and guarded.

'Then I'll come.' She prepared to get out of the car.

Grey's hand on her arm stopped her, stilled her

heart for just a moment before the silly thing galloped off at a faster rate than before. Just from a touch.

'You have a calming influence on me.' He drew a tight breath and blew it out. 'I know I haven't been at my best since I met you, Sophia. And that kiss complicated things.'

'Yes.' What else was there to say? They made their way to the lift and rode to the tenth floor in silence.

'I should have asked what exactly you'll be doing here.' Not roving ten floors on foot, she hoped. Maybe she should have insisted he explain everything in more detail, but she sensed he needed to come to grips a step at a time.

'What I'll be doing is announcing a sudden, short vacation.' The lift doors slid open. Grey cast one final glance at her as he moved to step through them. 'I usually just take a week off between Christmas and New Year, when everything slows to a crawl anyway.'

'That's not much time for relaxation over the years.'

'I thought it was enough.' His shoulders stiffened as he stepped out of the lift. He hobbled as little as possible as heads nodded and people greeted him with respectful murmurs of 'Mr Barlow' and 'Good to see you, Mr Barlow' as he and Soph passed them.

His offices had an understated air of opulence. State-of-the-art equipment sat on fine quality desks. The paintings on the walls were real, the carpet thick and springy beneath their feet.

Soph also attracted her share of glances. So many faces, all of them people working to help make Grey's company a success. The extent of his prestige and power hit home to her here in the hub of his business empire.

'Come this way, Soph.' He took her arm, guided her into a set of spacious rooms.

Her heart tripped because, for the first time since they'd met, he'd called her *Soph*. She couldn't stop the flow of warm feeling that stole over her—settled inside her—as a result.

This wasn't just simple attraction any more, she realised with a sense of panic. She liked and admired him, wanted to explore his complexities, understand what drove him. None of which was a good or smart idea.

Grey entered the rooms after her, shut the door and closed them in together. A middle-aged woman sat at a desk in front of them and her glance was both professional and welcoming as she looked up from her work. 'Grey. It's good to see you up and on your feet. The department heads are gathered and waiting in the meeting room.'

She paused and Grey drew Soph forward.

'My temporary assistant, Sophia Gable, this is my office assistant, Mrs Hilary Stubbs.'

'Hello.' Conscious of Grey's hand still at her back, Soph forced her attention to his assistant, smiled, noted the assessment in the other woman's gaze, but had no idea how she fared in the face of it. She did her share of assessing and decided that Mrs Stubbs looked efficient.

'There are two department heads missing. They were out of town, but they're adequately represented.' The woman reached for a stenographer's pad.

Grey waved a hand. 'I won't need you this time.' He moved closer and gave some instructions Soph didn't fully take in—something about a memo and management during his absence.

Soph couldn't seem to shift her attention from his closeness. She wanted to hug him, or at least offer him a nice calming bath and some incense candles. He wasn't exactly relaxed right now. Well, he would hate this, wouldn't he? Having to delegate, even if only for a while.

See? It's not so easy, is it? Say you wouldn't feel the same in his shoes.

Soph chewed on her lip.

His assistant started to type quickly on her computer keyboard.

Grey guided Soph into the conference room with him. Faces ranged up and down the sides of the long rectangular table. Soph snapped out of her musings and whispered in a hushed and urgent tone, 'Do *I* take notes? I don't have anything—'

'You don't have to do anything.' His fingers

tightened against her back for a moment before he dropped his hand. 'Just—I just want you here.' And then, gruffly, 'I don't fancy you as a suspect executive car thief, so I couldn't really leave you outside.'

But she knew that was just a foil. He wanted her presence. Soph went all mushy inside again.

She walked with Grey to the head of the table, slipped into the seat at his right when he indicated she should do so and noted the clamp of his jaw as he examined the faces of each of his senior staff members. Her mush factor gave way to concern for him.

'I'm taking a brief leave of absence from the company.' His announcement brought surprise to every face in the room. 'A short holiday, that's all, to…rest up.'

He glanced her way. 'An agency provided Sophia to assist me, drive my car and so forth.'

Many of those faces had turned to gaze speculatively at her, and Grey had taken care to make their relationship plain. It was both a kind and gentlemanly thing for him to do.

Before Soph could do more than offer a tentative smile, her boss drew an almost inaudible breath and went on. 'In my absence, you're all in charge of and fully responsible for all the projects in your separate departments. If there's an absolute emergency—

and I'm talking epic proportions when I say this—you can contact me. Otherwise, sort it out yourselves. You have the necessary training and abilities and I know I can…trust your judgement.'

Soph doubted anyone else would have noticed his infinitesimal hesitation, but she did.

He glanced at two nervous-looking individuals towards the end of the table. 'In your cases, you'll pass this on to your seniors.'

'Yes, sir.'

'Yes, Mr Barlow.'

Grey nodded and made eye contact with two men to his left. 'McCarty and Coates, please remain behind. The rest of you are dismissed. Thank you for your attendance and I'll let you know when my status changes. There'll be a memo today about…arrangements in my absence.'

The moment the door closed after the last person, the two middle-aged men turned to Grey. He held up a hand to stay any questions. 'I apologise that I've given you no notice about this, but I need you to stand in my stead in an overall management capacity while I'm gone.

'Shuffle responsibility for your projects as necessary, except for Beacon's Cove. You'll take care of that together. Make what decisions—jointly—that you have to. When I return to my duties, I'll expect a full report. Do your best to make it a positive one. Hilary will release a statement about your standing to all the relevant staff.'

'I appreciate the opportunity.' Coates seemed to straighten even more in his chair.

McCarty nodded. 'I'll do everything in my power to ensure that good report.'

'Thank you.' Grey stood from the table and reached for Soph's arm.

She rose and moved instinctively closer to him.

He dipped his head as the men murmured their farewells. 'I'll be in touch.'

Then, with his fingers wrapped around her arm and the muscles in his body so tightly locked that Soph could have bounced concrete off him, Grey moved to the door and scanned and quickly signed the single sheet of paper his office assistant held out to him.

As they exited the building, Soph gave vent to her questions. 'How long will you stop work completely? Can you trust those two men to run things? Will there be financial consequences as a result of your withdrawal—?'

'I can take a step back for a short time. Naturally I'd prefer things to go well while I do that, but I can't...make that happen.' He continued moving towards the car.

No, but maybe he would discover that he could trust his employees and their assurances and dedication?

'So you only need to do that? Take a break and everything will right itself and stay righted?' That was the other concern and, in her eyes, the even more important one. She searched his face as she waited for his answer.

'I'm off for the remainder of the week, then Doc Cooper will re-examine me.' His frown darkened. 'It had better be enough.' He sighed as they arrived at the car. 'Let's go back to the town house, Sophia.'

And Soph sighed. Was this a complete acknowledgement on his part? Or a small capitulation that he hoped would be enough, but might prove not to be?

CHAPTER SEVEN

'I'M SURE there are heaps of relaxing things you'd like to do over the next few days, using your country house retreat as a base.' When Grey simply glanced at her blankly, Soph forged on. She wanted to get him enthused, or at least help him to accept his immediate fate. That much would be one small step in the right direction, wouldn't it? 'Maybe some small trips during the day, a bit of local touristy stuff…'

Kissing your temporary assistant.

No. She didn't want him to do that again.

Yes, you do.

They were seated on comfy outdoor chairs on the balcony of Grey's town house with a view over the back garden and of some magnificent portions of the Melbourne skyline.

Soph had Alfie in her arms. It was really hard to sit here beside Grey and not desire him, because she did, and she felt closer to him emotionally thanks to all that had happened today, which was dangerous and quite probably dumb.

But she'd seen his vulnerability, had watched him hand over control of his company to others, even when he hadn't wanted to do it. Now, hours later, he was still struggling to accept what he had had to do. She could feel that, sense it, but somehow even that struggle drew her closer to him.

'Is there anything touristy to do other than climb in the mountains?' He didn't turn to look at her, but she felt his attention locked on her anyway. 'I suppose we can look into that when we go back tomorrow.'

'Yes, that will be soon enough.' Soph stroked Alfie's soft fur as she examined Grey's profile, so strong, and so stark right now. She'd seen that expression on her sister Bella's face at times over the years, when Bella had been worried but determined to hug her fears to herself.

'A lot of companies run successfully with a group of people to control their various areas, don't they?' She wanted to encourage him. 'Sometimes people like a chance to prove themselves. Maybe your staff will surprise you.'

Well, Soph could contribute to help Grey in ways she hadn't managed for her sisters. Now, in her new independent life, she wanted Grey to trust her with his feelings and his difficulties. Yes, she really did want that.

Warnings ricocheted around in her mind even as these thoughts came, but here, with the city around them and Grey so close at her side, Soph couldn't seem to think beyond his nearness.

'You think I've micromanaged when it wasn't necessary.' He did turn his head then, and let those fathomless green eyes pierce her.

Soph tipped her face up to the sky. 'I think you're trying to come to terms with your doctor being right about your stress levels, and you're furious about it and feel trapped by circumstances you can't control.'

'I haven't turned my back on the company since the day it became my responsibility. My father left me with three stepmothers to support financially. The money for their stipends comes out of company funds and he didn't stint in his generosity.' The words seemed to force their way out of him, low and intense. He sucked in a breath of air. 'The company employees also rely on me, upwards of five hundred people, one way and another. If I fail, they all pay for it. Maybe I've felt that if I'm in ultimate control at least I'll only have myself to blame if things go wrong.'

'I don't think you could be a failure if you tried.' He was too strong for that, strong inside and out, no matter what his physical condition might be right now.

'But you still think I have control issues.'

She hesitated because she didn't quite know how to deny it.

Grey got to his feet, held out his good hand to her. 'It doesn't matter. Let's go inside. I hadn't realised the amount of time we'd passed, just sitting here. I think we should order a meal. I'm not sure if there's much worth scrounging in my fridge or freezer or cupboards, and it's close to dinner time.'

Soph took Grey's hand, got to her feet. The movement brought her close to his big, muscled body, to the taut face that made her want to reach up, stroke and sooth, and touch him for the sheer pleasure of it.

She was overly aware of him, of the blunted scent of his cologne as it drifted to her on the evening air, of the crisp dark hair that seemed to beg her to run her fingers through it. Soph *did* want those things, could be so tempted to reach for them if he showed even the slightest interest in pursuing that path.

Then where would she be? Abandoned by him, that was where, because he wouldn't want more than an uninvolved few moments.

Soph stepped away from him, preceded him into the living room and waited while he closed and locked the balcony doors.

He subsided on to the sofa and positioned his foot on an ottoman for elevation. 'There's a restaurant menu stuck to the fridge door with a magnet. Will you order for us and pick us out a bottle of wine from my selection?'

She ran him a bath and he took that while they waited for the food to arrive. Then they ate and talked about nothing much. It felt weird and good all at once. Grey skimmed through a magazine while she took Alfie outside for a break.

Soph had helped Grey with a final set of physio exercises for the day and they were sipping a small second glass each of red wine side by side on the sofa when a hiccup burst out of her. She clapped a hand over her mouth and heat crept into her cheeks. 'I'm sorry—how embarrassing.'

Grey laughed. It was the first time the tension had truly left him all day, and something inside Soph fluttered into life. The press of his leg against hers now became something more than incidental, the look in his eyes deeper than simple interest in their conversation.

Please, Grey. Don't make me notice how wonderful you look when you smile, don't make me so aware of your nearness. I'm having enough trouble already.

She stuttered into speech—anything to dissipate the tension suddenly inside her, on his face, all around them. 'My sisters say I have no palate, but I chose a nice wine from your selection, don't you think?'

Grey's gaze dipped to her mouth, then rose to her eyes. 'I enjoyed the wine.'

'And you had it in moderation.' Soph was pretty

much a one glass wonder herself and, with their two small servings, they'd had about that.

Grey needed to change the subject to something that would take his mind off wanting to kiss Sophia. Discussing her family seemed a safe choice.

'You could visit your sisters in the morning before we leave the city.' He didn't quite manage to shift his gaze from Sophia's softly flushed face. 'I figure you would like to see them, as you all seem to be close. I've noticed lots of text messages flying to and fro.'

Grey never indulged in voluntary family gatherings.

'That's very nice of you.' Her words were appreciative. 'I don't think I'd feel comfortable leaving you to amuse yourself when it's my job to do that, but if you felt you might enjoy the visit we could go together.'

That wasn't what he had meant. But she watched him with such hope on her face that he opened his mouth and agreed before he could stop himself.

'I guess that would be okay.' And then he justified his decision. 'I'll be relying on you to find ways to keep me occupied. Enforced leisure isn't something I have any familiarity with. A visit to your family will use my time as well as anything else.'

'I guess so.' She sobered a little at that, but then

that generous smile slipped through again. 'Let me call my sister, make the arrangements. I'll do my best to keep you busy, and you'll probably enjoy meeting Bella and Chrissy. They're really great people.'

Grey just wanted to work hard, as he had for as long as he could remember. As for relaxing, could he do that with Sophia? With the way he still wanted her? 'Make the visit for about ten-thirty tomorrow morning, if that will suit them. It will give us time to buy some groceries first. You can make more healthy soup for me.'

'I'd like to do that.' Her gaze locked with his a little too long before she looked away. At his indication, she used the phone on the end stand beside the sofa to put in a quick call to one of her sisters, Grey wasn't sure which one.

Soph didn't have to move away from him as she made the call and he found he wanted her near. Her whole tone of voice changed as she talked, softened with a particular kind of affection that tugged at him.

A family that actually gave a damn about each other wasn't something he usually thought about. Until now he had accepted his history, had used it as an example of the mistakes he didn't want to make and accepted that most of the times he heard from his stepmothers they wanted something.

Oh, they cared about him in their own ways, he supposed. He cared about them. They were his father's past wives. How could he not? But it wasn't the same as what Soph had.

Yet why start examining all that now? Looking at it wouldn't change anything, and he had accepted his limitations and his family's limitations long ago.

Soph ended the call. The rabbit chose that moment to come to life where it sat on the floor near her feet. It sat up on its haunches, twitched its nose and dipped its head up and down, then sniffed the carpet, tried to chew on it and gave up and settled back into a boneless lump beside Sophia's feet.

With a soft laugh, she lifted the rabbit into her arms. As she cuddled the furry blob she crooned to it in a soft, sweet voice. 'I'm so glad I found you, Alfred. You're just so special.'

She was doting on a rabbit, and why that should underscore his attraction to her Grey could not have explained, but it did.

'At least it hasn't had any accidents.' While Grey stared at Soph and recited all the reasons he shouldn't want her, she glanced up at him.

Her gaze lingered, linked with his and held. 'You're really quite tolerant of Alfie.'

'I don't know why you think that.' But Grey admitted that he wanted to be cuddled and crooned to by her. Not pampered, not because he had injuries.

He wanted Sophia's softness, her sweetness and openness, all for him, a man who couldn't be more closed off emotionally if he tried. He'd set out to be that way and he'd succeeded. Yet the desire stayed with him.

'I think it because it's true.' She eased the rabbit back on to the floor and locked her hands together in her lap. Too damned close—close enough for Grey to touch her, and he did. His fingers lifted, brushed the soft nape of her neck. He couldn't stop himself.

Their faces were so close. He could smell the tang of wine on her breath, could imagine kissing it from her lips. Frustration clawed at him, undermining his control again. He'd been forced to give up his working life, even if only for now. The doctor had snapped at him and treated him like a baby and accused him of having too much ego and not enough sense.

Overall it had been an irritating, frustrating day and just for once he would like to have what he wanted. And what he wanted…was Sophia. He wanted her more than he cared to admit, in so many ways.

'G-Grey?' Her eyes widened as she searched his face and tension whirled around them.

He should stay the heck away from her, but he wasn't sure if he could. Grey closed his fingers around that soft nape and exerted just enough pressure to bring her closer. 'I know what I said this morning, but I want to kiss you again, Sophia, and I think you want me to.'

A second kiss. What could it matter if they both agreed?

If this was self-delusion, he didn't want to know about it.

'Maybe I do want it, but…' The words were a mere whisper. Her gaze locked with his. Her lush mouth was soft and inviting.

Her lashes fluttered. He imagined them against his skin. His fingers tightened and he fought himself, forced the words to come because she had to decide.

'You can tell me goodnight, Sophia.' He wanted her in his bed, under him, wanted her in every way imaginable, but right now, in this moment, he wanted her kiss.

She drew a slow, deep breath that did stunning things to her curves and made his body clench with need. 'I…don't want to say it yet.'

Grey let out a low growl and drew her up close to him because if he was doing this he was taking everything he could, and he let their mouths fuse.

He knew the taste of her now and once he had it again he didn't want to stop. Instead, with her cooperation clear in each sigh, each press of soft lips to his, he dived headlong and recklessly forward, sensible thought far away, subjugated by want.

And perhaps need.

That last was truly worrying, but he pushed the worry aside and focused on the feel of her clasped close to him, the soft curves of her body and the sweet giving of her mouth.

Their bodies merged, two parts that fitted as though made for each other. He forgot his injuries and simply held her as he absorbed every nuance of this. Of Sophia—warm and sweet and seductive in his hold.

She wrapped her arm around his neck, pressed against him. Her fingers trembled against his nape. Emotion caught in her eyes and stirred in him.

Something yielded inside Grey then. He couldn't explain it and didn't want to think about it, but he had to have her. Close to him, as much as he could take, as much as she would give and he could give back to her. He didn't know how much that was and couldn't try to figure it out.

The cast was a barrier. He made up for it by exploring her face and neck with his lips until she shivered in his arms. Need pressed behind his eyelids, filled his fingertips, climbed his spinal column to settle at the base of his neck where her fingers touched him.

Her soft murmurs of approval urged him on. He cupped her arm, her shoulder, her waist and finally her breast through the cloth of her blouse and the silken bra beneath. Grey moaned and deepened their kiss, and her hands slid to his chest in a return of the caress he had instigated.

In moments or aeons—he was too lost to know

which—they were pressed back into the sofa, bodies entwined. Hands tugged at buttons while soft sighs and urgent murmurs led to deeper kisses, to more—just more of everything.

Grey had Sophia beneath him, all of his senses engaged in one need. He wanted to bring them together utterly. Brown eyes met his gaze, wide and mellow and welcoming. He buried his face in her neck and leaned both arms down without thinking.

The pain was instant, though quickly ended as he reared back.

'Have you hurt it?' Soph came forward on to her knees on the sofa even as he sat back. Concern for him and desire both mingled in her gaze.

'I don't think so. I just forgot.' They probably both knew why he'd forgotten. As the fog of hunger and need cleared away, he confronted the reality of what had almost happened here. There were reasons it shouldn't have.

He'd fallen into madness and almost taken her with him—straight to his bed for a night of lovemaking. Actually, he wasn't sure he'd have made it even that far before he claimed her.

And then what? He didn't have anything to offer beyond a temporary physical joining or a number of them, and that kind of offer could hardly be fair to her.

He gritted his teeth. 'This is my fault. I let desire cloud my thinking. Go to bed, Sophia. Go to bed and be glad something stopped me. I can't care for you the way you would need. It's not…I don't have those feelings inside me and I don't want to hurt you with anything else.'

Soph stared at Grey and struggled to pull herself together. He had taken her apart with his kisses, with the strength of his desire for her, and she had let him.

She tried to absorb what had happened, what hadn't. Her feelings about both of those things. Her feelings towards Grey were changing. She knew that much. They *had* changed and beyond those changes lay the temptation, pure and simple, to have what she could have of him and with him, for however long it might last. Would it be so bad if she reached out for only that?

Couldn't she guard herself from hurt? Take precautions with her feelings?

She didn't know any more and now wasn't the time to try to sort it out. So, instead, she got to her feet and walked silently to her room. She didn't agree with Grey or disagree, because she no longer knew what she believed.

It was only when she reached her door and hesitated, glancing back over her shoulder, that she saw the rabbit had followed her, had hopped along behind her.

Soph bent to scoop Alfie into her arms, but for the first time she found little comfort in holding him as the realisation came.

Grey had rejected her. He might have couched it as care for her, but in the end he had stopped, had turned from her. He clearly hadn't wanted her enough to go on.

CHAPTER EIGHT

'IF THE cars in the driveway are any indication, your family gathering seems to have expanded to include more than your two sisters.' After nodding to Luc and Bella's housekeeper/nanny as she invited them in, Grey murmured the words against Soph's ear. They stepped inside the house.

Grey had been…odd this morning. Solicitous, as they'd found a grocery store and stocked up on necessities for their return to his country house. Determined to be relaxed, even as he'd dived on the papers at the grocery store checkout stand and purchased every one of them with an air of suppressed relief. He had then proceeded to snort and grumble his way through the business sections as Soph had driven them towards Bella's home.

If she offered Grey an affair, would he take it? Would she really want him to? Soph hadn't magically found the answers between last night and this morning. 'It does look as though my brothers-in-law are here.' She shifted Alfie slightly in her arms and hoped Bella wouldn't mind the addition of a rabbit at their morning tea.

'Go on in now. I'll get the tea for everyone.' The housekeeper smiled and bustled away.

Soph led the way to the living room. She wasn't particularly surprised to see not only Bella and Chrissy, but their husbands, Luc and Nate, Nate's grandfather Henry, and Nate and Chrissy's baby daughter Anastasia in the room. Her family loved and supported her. She'd made a change in her work life; this was their chance to meet her current employer in person.

Enough said. Except for the fact that she wanted Grey to take a good look at these people, see what family was really about. Why would she want that? So he would be impressed and want the same thing with her?

No. And not going to happen, anyway.

Her family all gazed at her expectantly from various parts of the room. Grey stood still and tense at her side.

'It's great to see you all. As you can see, Alfie the rescued rabbit is doing well.' Soph drew a steadying breath and hoped her family hadn't noticed her distraction. 'And this is my current employer through the agency, Grey Barlow.' Did her voice soften as she said Grey's name? Soph's fingers curled more securely about Alfie's soft fur.

'Sophia, it's great to see you. Are you well?' The words came from Bella before she stepped forward and enveloped Soph and the rabbit in a hug, at which point she added in a low tone, 'You really are comfortable in your job with this man? Because if you're not—'

'I like the job.' *And I like the man. I like the man more and more.* Soph squeezed her eldest sister back and, as they drew apart, smiled at her. 'I'm having an adventure, one employment opportunity at a time.'

That was how it had started, and yet it seemed so much beyond that now.

Bella relaxed a little, and Soph introduced her eldest sister to Grey. She then introduced Bella's husband Luchino, Chrissy and her husband Nate, who grinned as he watched his daughter spider-crawl around the room at lightning speed. Henry Montbank, Nate's grandfather, reclined comfortably in a chair.

The only one missing was Luc's daughter, Grace, who would be at school at this hour. Grey dipped his head, offered low greetings in return. His hand splayed against the centre of Soph's back in that familiar way, and that added to her shivery factor—whether she should let it, or not.

Did he realise he was touching her? Was it because he felt out of place, or for other reasons?

Bella noticed, of course. Her eyes narrowed and her gaze moved from one to the other of them and back again while Chrissy watched them silently.

Since Soph didn't want an epic-sized sisterly inquisition, she rushed into speech. 'Um, if I put the rabbit down do you think Anastasia will try to chew on him? I found the poor thing tied to a pole near my apartment the evening before I started work with Grey. Abandoned. The rabbit, I mean. It appalled me, but Joe had the collapsible cage and I scrounged some pellets from a neighbour…' She ran out of words.

Chrissy came over and bestowed her own gentle hug. 'Anastasia *will* probably want to get up close and personal with the rabbit, but we'll deal with it if it becomes a problem.'

'Come in, anyway. Sit down. We'll have our tea.' Bella led the way into the room with the model's walk that would never leave her. The housekeeper had slipped in with the tea so quietly that Soph hadn't noticed.

Bella now offered tea or coffee, cake and cookies. 'The tea is a Chai blend but we can get some regular if that's better.'

This was for Grey's benefit, no doubt, as everyone else knew that Bella always drank Chai, and Chrissy and Soph were partial.

So they had morning tea. Luc and Nate talked business with Grey. Luc had a forthcoming auction in progress for the purchase of some rare Australian gemstones. Nate bemoaned the need to head overseas for a brief stint to settle some shipping business that required his personal touch.

Henry Montbank tossed in the occasional comment, his eyes alight with interest. Soph started out speaking quietly with her sisters but soon they were laughing and teasing, swapping anecdotes, the latest bits of news.

Grey was reserved at first, but how could he remain stiff and formal while a baby chased a rabbit around the room, and the rabbit then surprised everyone by chasing the baby? As Alfie hopped after Anastasia, determined, it seemed, to keep up with her, Soph grinned.

'I guess I can stop worrying that the baby might traumatise your rabbit.' Chrissy smiled. 'He doesn't seem inclined to let her get her hands on him, but he appears to like playing chase with her.'

'Yes, I hadn't expected Alfie to do any of the chasing.' Soph grinned and pulled her niece into her arms for a cuddle as she started to crawl past her.

She and Grey were side by side on the couch, something that had somehow occurred in the flurry when they had all taken their seats. His thigh pressed against hers, as it had last night.

The man sat too close, that was the problem. She could hear every breath he took, and all of it affected her on some deep, impossible level she struggled to comprehend, let alone control.

To hide her consternation, Soph bent her head and kissed Anastasia's downy one.

Only when she looked up did she find Grey's stormy eyes locked on to her. The smile had washed from his face, replaced by something startled and uncomfortable and hungry and a little horrified. For just a moment years of loneliness—and his unwillingness to have anything to do with all of this—shone in his eyes.

Soph felt incredibly sad for him in that moment.

His mother had died. Three stepmothers had allowed him to slip away from them one after another when the pressure had been on and his father had no longer wanted them. Soph guessed that his father might not have been as supportive as he could have been, either. Otherwise, wouldn't he have done something to protect Grey better as a child?

How could Grey come back from those repeated losses? He'd built his self-sufficiency and his control and his singleness strongly. He held fast to them.

And, without truly realising it, Soph had allowed herself to hope just a little…

Well, that had been stupid. She didn't want any of that, anyway.

Anastasia yawned and burrowed her head into the crook of Soph's neck, and Soph kissed her niece's curls again and patted the little girl's back. She didn't want to think any more.

Grey shifted beside her, a discomfited movement.

'Are you in pain?' She turned her head to look at him, whispering the words so they wouldn't be overheard.

'No.' His gaze roved again over her and the baby. 'No, I'm fine.'

'How long do you expect to have Sophia with you, Grey?' Bella spoke, her gaze thoughtful as it moved from one to the other of them.

'We're all behind our sister's career change and we appreciate you taking time so Soph could visit us today.' Chrissy added her contribution to the conversation. 'We're keen to know she's happy and comfortable in her new role.'

Soph had thought she'd headed off the inquisition permanently. She should have known better, and she recognised these seemingly innocent queries for what they were.

If she let them keep on, they would. Why should they question Grey, anyway? He was a perfectly good employer—the best.

'I certainly am happy in my new role.' Soph got to her feet, warm, sleepy baby pressed to her neck and chest. 'Speaking of my job, we should go, shouldn't we, Grey? There are perishables in the car that will only last so long in their cool-box.' To her sisters she explained, 'We shopped for groceries before we came here.'

Grey's expression when he rose was so deadpan that she just *knew* he'd seen straight through Bella and Chrissy's polite words to the *you'd better be nice to our sister* warnings veiled beneath. So long as he hadn't seen Soph's thoughts!

She handed Anastasia to Chrissy and scooped Alfie from the floor and into her arms instead. 'I promised Grey vegetable lasagne surprise for dinner. It will need to bake for most of the afternoon, so we'd better move along.'

'I look forward to the meal. If it's like all your others, it will be memorable.' Grey's hand rested again in the small of her back, this time as he propelled her towards the door. When he went on his voice held a little surprise. 'It's odd. I usually enjoy food I order in from the restaurant near my home, but even though you ordered dishes I've had from there before, I found it kind of bland last night.'

Grey seemed to remember the rest of the evening at the same time that it flashed once more through Soph's mind. Would they ever forget it? He fell silent.

Everyone else had too, right about the time of his first mention of food.

'You'll keep in contact?' Bella finally said.

'As always. Give me a hug goodbye.' Soph reached for her sister.

Bella held her tightly and bent to whisper in her ear, 'I know you're all grown up, just…if you need anything, or if anything is worrying you or…I don't know, if you just want…'

'I know. I love you, too. He's a *good* employer, Bella. I want to be with him.' She wanted that, and she loved her sisters so much. Soph tightened her hold. 'I would do anything for you and Chrissy, anything in the whole world.' The words just burst out.

'But we're fine…' Bella drew back and searched her face, but Chrissy was there, waiting to exchange goodbyes. Soph hugged her other sister and felt oddly choked up and so she said nothing more and hugged her brothers-in-law and Henry.

Grey stood silently waiting for her until they went outside and the ache in her chest slowly eased away.

'They…uh…sometimes my sisters are a little protective.' She uttered the words as they made their way out of the city limits. This was something she could explain.

Right now, Soph appreciated anything she even slightly understood. 'Truly, you don't need to think anything of it. Sometimes Bella used to even forget herself and interrogate Joe when he came to take me out somewhere.'

A sharp green gaze turned her way. 'Joe?'

'He's the mechanic who lives and works near my

apartment.' Lovely Joe who looked as if he might have found someone after such a long time alone and, oh, Soph hoped it worked out for him. 'He's been a special friend to me and my sisters for years.'

'I'd like to meet him one day.' Grey seemed surprised by his words. He fell silent for a few moments. 'Maybe your sisters *should* be worried about me.'

'Nothing's changed.' All sorts of things had, but not the things that defined how their relationship had to be. 'We both don't want to be involved.' She had toyed with the idea of an affair. She acknowledged now that it would be dangerous for her because some feelings had developed.

None too scary, just a softening inside her that could end in pain if she didn't take care, didn't protect herself. 'We won't let things get out of hand again, that's all.'

She forced what she hoped looked like a bright smile. 'I'm looking forward to making the lasagne. They had a good fresh vegetable selection at the supermarket, didn't you think?'

They hit the country road and she went on to bring a discussion of carrots and broccoli and cabbage and cauliflower to new levels of stupefaction.

And Grey let her. Maybe he also found that easier.

'I made a conference phone call to Coates and McCarty while you were busy in the kitchen.' Grey uttered the words as he leaned back on his elbow on the picnic blanket.

They were surrounded by meadow grass and wild flowers, bathed in late afternoon sunshine. Not a great distance from the house—they could see it clearly from here—but Soph had driven him so he didn't have to walk over the uneven ground. The car waited in a dip not far away.

This was relaxation 101, Sophia Gable style. So far, he wasn't as fed up as he had expected to be. Tense, yes, but in a different way that had nothing to do with stress levels.

Grey suppressed a frustrated snort and settled for tugging up a blade of grass. He rolled it through his fingers. 'Everything is going well, including the Beacon's Cove project. I shouldn't need to be in contact again until after the doctor approves me to return to Melbourne for the duration.'

That should happen about three days from now. It had *better* happen then.

Grey glanced up at a perfect blue sky and wanted to look at Soph instead.

'We'll have a really peaceful time of it, Grey. You'll enjoy it, truly. The change of pace will be good for you.' She leaned forward, her legs curled under her, and he let himself look, just a little, just enough to indulge a need he shouldn't have.

'I hope you haven't made many other calls to do

with your work.' Before he had a chance to be annoyed, she went on. 'You might like to know I've made some plans for tomorrow, now that I've aced you with the crossword puzzles in the papers.' Her eyes danced as she said it.

Alerted and intrigued, Grey sat up. The movement brought their bodies very close. 'First of all, you didn't ace me with the crossword puzzles; I let you help me and together we completed them all.'

She copied one of his snorts and grinned, and he wanted to kiss her.

'What plans have you made for tomorrow, Sophia?' He watched while the lovely face flushed and her breath caught. Not because she had a secret, but because their gazes had locked and something unbidden had flared between them yet again.

Her gaze dropped away from his and she mumbled her answer towards the multicoloured blanket beneath them. 'Wouldn't you rather be surprised? You gave me free rein to figure out how to make the time pass for you.'

'I don't seem to remember that conversation.' Indeed, Grey remembered no such thing because it hadn't happened. 'In fact, I said I'd get on the Internet and find some suitable occupations for myself.

'Maybe some online courses in short business topics. And I distinctly remember saying I could help you in the kitchen and we could take an inventory of the house and plan how to redecorate it since the furnishings are a few years old now.'

'The house is perfect exactly as it is.' She glared at him as she had when he'd first made the suggestion. 'It's homely and reflects your personality, if you must know.'

That punched the grin off his face and punched him in the gut at the same time. She knew how to deliver a verbal blow that would knock him off his high ropes, didn't she?

What exactly did he want of her?

The answer to that was both simple and complicated. Nothing he could have, nothing he should ask for. Nothing that could last for longer than the time they had together, and that just wouldn't be enough.

For Soph. *It wouldn't be enough for Soph.*

Yeah? So why did you try to get her to play house with you—something you've never done with a woman in your life?

He hadn't. He'd been searching for ways to occupy himself!

She waved a hand. 'At any rate, I'd rather keep tomorrow as a surprise. It will give you something to anticipate.'

'You think so?' He leaned forward, just close enough to inhale the scent of her.

Delicate shoulders beneath the orange cheesecloth blouse tightened into immobility as their bodies all but brushed. She swallowed. 'Um…'

His hand rose. He clasped her shoulder, gritting his teeth as his body absorbed her nearness, the sweet, lovely scent of her, the touch of soft cloth and the knowledge of softer skin beneath it.

She couldn't seem to shift her gaze from him. Instead, she lifted her free hand to fiddle with the garland of wild flowers around her neck.

His gaze followed. Naturally. He let his head bend towards hers as the bands of control loosened and slipped. 'You're torturing me.'

Soph's head lifted at the same time. Her fingers gripped his shoulder. 'You're doing it to me—more.'

'This won't mean anything,' he cautioned. 'And I won't take it too far.'

Her chin tipped up. 'Nobody asked you to make it mean anything, or to be my keeper.'

'I warned you.' But the warning was to himself, really, and he couldn't heed it anyway.

Instead, he closed the distance, closed his lips over hers, took one deep, lingering taste. There was nothing special here, nothing to lift this above any other intimacy he had experienced, he assured himself.

Her taste put the lie to that assurance immediately, exploded on his tongue, burst through him and flooded him. Everywhere. Senses, nerve-endings, *feelings*.

She drew back before he was ready. Her eyes were wide, the lush mouth soft and vulnerable.

Grey felt…almost overwhelmed. What was wrong with him? What had happened to the feelings he had guarded so well and that now were in disarray, fractured all through him until he didn't know what he wanted any more?

Before Grey could work it out, if that was even possible, a sound impinged. It took moments for his mind to clear enough to recognise the noise as cars, more than one, approaching on the road that led to the house.

He glanced over his shoulder in time to see those cars, three of them, draw to a halt outside his home. An involuntary groan escaped him.

'What's the matter?' Soph followed his gaze and stared, as Grey did, at the flotilla of three brightly coloured convertibles that now sat outside his house.

Metallic blue. Fire engine red. Flashy green. Three women emerged from those cars, each dressed in colours to match. As one they swarmed on the house, knocked on the door and waited, and moments later, after dismantling one of his window-frames and putting it back again, disappeared inside.

'Are we being burgled in primary colours?' Soph murmured the words but, even as she said it, he watched her put it together in her head. 'Those are your stepmothers, aren't they? How did they know to get inside the house like that?'

'I once advised them that if they insisted on leaving a key outside their homes, the inside of a window-frame was a better place than under the mat.' He shouldn't have done such a thing, himself, but this was the middle of nowhere. He'd considered it safe enough.

'No doubt they've decided we've gone away somewhere, and chosen to wait inside in comfort until we get back.' All he wanted was to forget their presence and go back to kissing Soph, but look where that had got him. A whole lot of frustration, and an even greater urge to make her his and damn the consequences and the future and any guilt or caution he might feel.

'Do you want to go somewhere? Want to avoid them? You assigned me your protector from visitors when I first started with you.' She sat up, that protectiveness there in full glory for him to see. And appreciate, even though he didn't need it.

She was cute and sweet and desirable when she wanted to look out for him. It made him want to protect *her* twice as much. Trouble was, he appeared to be her worst enemy at the moment.

Soph chewed that luscious lower lip of hers. 'If their presence will make you stressed—'

'They won't make me stressed.' They may have

just saved him from doing something really, really stupid, though, and, despite the fact that Soph had been the first to draw away, he knew she would have let him.

He rose awkwardly to his feet and held out his hand to help her up. His fingers continued to grip hers for a moment after she stood and then he made himself let go. 'Shall we go meet them?'

'Together.' She spoke it as a decree.

Grey smiled, though he had no idea what he had to smile about. 'Yes, we'll go together.'

CHAPTER NINE

'LEANNA, Sharon, Dawn. I'm surprised to see you all here.' Grey spoke the words in a quiet tone.

Soph searched the faces in front of them, all of them surprised, a little guilty. The stepmothers all rushed forward and then stopped just shy of touching him.

'You are all right, Grey?'

'Your injuries are recovering as they should?'

'The country air and isolation are helping you?'

Soph thought the latter was kind of moot right now, but she softened a little at the concern in each face before it was carefully masked and the women began to chatter as they had over the phone—about trips and borrowing company transportation and paying off overdue bills.

'My injuries are healing as expected,' he answered when they finally all came up for air.

Grey gestured towards the sofa and chairs. 'I would have checked on you all when I returned to Melbourne, but now that you're here…'

They all sat. Thanked him. Explained their problems in detail and looked at him expectantly as though waiting for his answers. It almost seemed as though they found a secure familiarity in bringing their troubles to his door.

Grey settled on to the sofa and Soph sat beside him. He glanced towards her. Let his arm brush against hers. She drew a deep breath and sighed it out again. She truly had totally and utterly no idea what she was going to do.

'This is Sophia Gable, my assistant while I'm recovering.' He glanced towards each stepmother in turn. 'Sophia, these are Sharon, Dawn and Leanna, my late father's ex-wives.'

Nods and hellos were exchanged.

'Would you make some tea, Soph?' Grey's thigh pressed against hers as he asked the question.

In the moment it took for Soph to shift her attention from that touch, he went on, 'Actually, could we have cardamom coffee? Would it take long? And maybe some of those interesting cookies you made last night?'

'I'll do it now.' Though she didn't want to leave him, he probably wanted to answer his stepmothers' questions privately. He'd called her Soph again too. She liked it far too much when he did that.

Soph got to her feet. She would prepare the food and if she heard raised voices or anything she would come to his rescue. 'I'll be back in a few minutes, but if you need me—'

'Don't tempt me.' He spoke the words in a low rumble none of the others would have heard.

Soph's jaw dropped and she scuttled off like a…rabbit, conscious that any distance she may have thought she had gained since they'd returned from the meadow had disappeared.

Grey couldn't keep the smile quite at bay as he watched Sophia's backside swish all the way to the kitchen. Eventually he turned his gaze back to his stepmothers, who all observed him with differing degrees of interest and curiosity in the depths of their guarded eyes.

In fact, they were always guarded around him, and he around them, and it only just hit him that this was so as he compared that behaviour to Soph's utter openness and to what his stepmothers used to be like, once upon a time. Well, Soph wasn't always an open book, but she was about some things.

A sigh passed through his lips. He listened to Soph clang things around in the kitchen and decided to get this over with before she came back. She seemed determined to protect him. Well, Grey had demanded she push any visitors off the doorstep, hadn't he, at the start. This was a little more complicated. It always felt complicated with the stepmothers.

'We've covered all this ground a number of times

in the past.' Even the opening gambit was well used. He went on anyway. 'Though I understand your concerns, I don't believe it's in anyone's best interests for me to pay off credit cards or pay other amounts outside your stipends. The company's equipment, the use of planes and such, my yacht, which is often reserved for business—those things are not available to any of you personally for good reason. Work is work, play isn't. So, basically, you all need to learn to live off your allowances.'

'Yes, you're right.'

'I know, dear. I will try harder.'

'Perfectly fair. I suppose I wasn't thinking when I asked for a charter plane.'

They accepted his response. They always did until the next time they brought up something similar. Grey didn't really understand this, but he didn't want to upset them, and maybe he could afford to bend a little?

'I'll tell you what. I'll have my solicitor pay some extra money into each of your accounts.' He named a figure. 'I won't make a habit of it, but that should tide you over. And I'll get each of you some financial counselling sessions as well. Perhaps then we won't have to go through this time and again.'

He gazed at each of them, expecting to at least see some relief, if nothing else.

The all looked disappointed.

'Oh, well, naturally you won't want to continue dealing with these matters—'

'I can manage. I don't need to see a financial counsellor—'

'I just like to consult with you…'

Soph came forward with the coffee and cookies on a tray then, and Grey mentally shook his head, confounded and not sure why. Maybe he was destined to feel that way since coming into contact with his confusing and desirable assistant?

The stepmothers sipped the coffee and nibbled the cookies and were oddly subdued. Indeed, they all seemed to have lost their appetites and set the food and drinks aside after just moments.

'I suppose we should be going.' Leanna got to her feet. The sparkle that had risen in her eyes when she'd first arrived and greeted him had disappeared again.

Dawn followed. 'We've disturbed your peace long enough.'

Sharon set down her coffee and slightly nibbled cookie as though glad to be rid of them. 'Thank you for seeing us. We'll…get out of your way.'

'I'll show you all out.' Soph stood.

Grey followed suit and they all moved to the front door while tension arced down his spine. He felt completely inadequate and bewildered.

'I really do need isolation.' He spoke the words

in uncharacteristic disclosure, but it was the only thing he could think of that might soothe this… ruffled impression he got from his stepmothers. 'The doctor has discovered elevated stress levels. I have to get them down and he feels if I'm alone out here it will give me the best chance.'

Leanna swung to face him. 'Your father didn't take proper care. I kept telling him he needed to—'

Dawn frowned. 'And your mother had that heart attack. We all know about that.'

'You need us to stay away.' Sharon seemed to say it for all of them. She drew herself up and gave a determined nod. 'We understand. What matters is that you get better. You won't be troubled again while you recover, Grey, be assured of that. In the meantime, please take care.'

'I…uh…I will.' Their obvious concern left him floundering again. When first Sharon and then Dawn leaned forward to kiss his cheek, Grey floundered more. Then Leanna patted his shoulder as she had done when he'd been a small boy missing his mother. He'd forgotten…

They left and Grey turned back to Sophia, making an excuse to get out of her company because he didn't know what he was doing any more. He didn't know at all, in any way, shape or form, and he really needed to get his head pulled back together. 'I think I'll take a nap before dinner.'

'I thought you might like to talk about your step-mothers. They all seemed quite concerned—'

'Yes. No. I mean…they did…but I don't need to talk about them.' His voice had a desperate edge that appalled him. He cleared his throat.

'You go to bed, then.' She gave the advice with a kind smile that made him grit his teeth. 'Everything will seem better once you've rested, you'll see.'

Just as though she was completely in control of her life and everything in it and not the slightest bit off-kilter as a result of what had happened out there in the meadow before they had been interrupted.

You mean you were interrupted when you were longing to make love to her.

Yes. Fine. He meant that. Grey stamped so hard on his good foot that it jarred all the way to the hip joint. 'I'm going to bed,' he growled and took the stairs at an irritated, uneven clip. Maybe he'd soak his head under the tap before his nap.

Would a blast of chilly water do anything to straighten out his thoughts?

Somehow, he doubted it.

She wore green nail polish and a glittery green scarf over her hair, *à la* that carefree woman who drove around in the vintage convertible and pretended to be a movie star. But Soph wasn't a movie star and, frankly, life didn't feel all that carefree from her viewpoint just at the moment.

Even Alfie had an unexpected problem. When she'd gone to return him to his cage this morning she'd found the covering blanket in a heap halfway across the yard. It had appeared to have been chewed.

The most probable cause was a straying farm dog or some other animal, and it meant Soph had to shut her pet safely in the big old shed, cage and all, to make sure he stayed safe while she and Grey weren't at the house.

Her rabbit didn't seem to mind too much. The shed had a high gate on the front, so at least Alfie wasn't locked away in the dark.

Soph sighed and turned her attention back to the moment. She had coloured portions of her hair green to match her scarf and nail polish. It was just a wash out. Blonde and green tips stuck out around the scarf and fluttered in the breeze and she should have felt powerful and in control of her world.

But she didn't.

They were at a wild flower farm about a forty minute drive from Grey's country home. This was day two of Grey relaxing utterly and detoxifying his stress levels—she hoped that would happen, anyway, despite the fact they'd been creeping around each other since the meadow incident and the stepmothers yesterday.

Well, today was a new day. Soph had driven up a narrow, winding road far into the mountains to get them here—some of it with only a flimsy guard rail between them and a great deal of free space below.

She mostly had experience of driving in Melbourne, yet she had given Grey breathtaking views, had made an effort, but, darn him, all he'd done was pull out his cheque book and pay the tour fee when they'd arrived and had not looked at her or shown either surprise or pleasure that she'd planned this treat to surprise him.

And did she want him to look when they couldn't do anything about the looking? She stifled a scream.

'You don't seriously expect me to climb on that thing and be carted all over the place?' Grey glanced at the odd piece of machinery a few feet away from them.

It was a morph somewhere between a quad bike and go-kart, with room to seat a driver up front and two behind. The farm owner waited patiently on it to take them on their tour.

'It'll be fun.' Soph hauled a pair of oversized sunglasses out of her tote bag, shoved them on to her nose and strolled forward.

She made sure she took her time so Grey could keep up on the uneven ground of the farm's main yard without any risk to his ankle. The way he'd taken the stairs yesterday before his nap, she'd worried he would hurt himself.

'Haven't you ever wondered about this particular industry? It's right on your doorstep, virtually. Now you'll know how it all works. We could buy some wild flowers. Make some dried arrangements for your place. I'm certain deep down you're pleased with your surprise.'

He stopped dead still in the middle of the yard and his face first tightened into a frown and then he cursed and came closer. 'I *am* pleased with the surprise. Thank you for thinking of it.'

Melt, melt.

That was her annoyance dribbling away and getting soaked up by the dry earth packed beneath their feet, not a starburst of happiness.

He moved past her and greeted the farm owner with a few polite words and a handshake and climbed aboard.

Soph caught up, but her heart took a little longer.

'All ready?' The man turned. He was young, around her age, and attractive in a rugged, outdoorsy way. 'My sister's busy in one of the sorting sheds, but you'll meet her later.' He gave Soph a slow, laconic, close up examination that ended in a toe-curling smile.

Grey bristled.

Soph returned the man's smile rather absently and wondered if, at another time, she might have been attracted by the deep countryman's drawl, the tanned face and a pair of sky-blue eyes fringed with thick brown lashes. All she could see, hear or feel with all her senses was Grey.

She sighed, whipped her tote bag open again, hauled out a cushion and plopped it under Grey's foot before he could do anything to prevent her. Well, that was what tote bags were for—carrying everything and the kitchen sink in case you wanted to use it. 'Ready. I look forward to learning all about your flower production.'

'From around April to after Christmas is the busiest time of year for us.' The man moved the vehicle forward and began to point out various sheds and buildings.

He drove them towards the panorama of flower-bedecked fields to the north. 'We produce fifteen different kinds of Australian native wild flowers and sell them to florists in Melbourne and to wholesalers throughout Australia. We also sell direct to a number of foreign markets.'

It took Grey about two minutes to get truly interested, three before he started to pepper the conversation with questions, and five before he sat bolt upright in his seat so he could see better.

Soph sighed and settled back to enjoy the tour.

They travelled around the outsides of some of the paddocks of flowers and viewed the sheds with materials in all stages of processing, but didn't come across the sister. At the end of the tour they stood in the foyer of a small cottage. The farmer handed them the biggest bunch of dried flowers Soph had ever seen.

'The flowers are on the house.' He shrugged. 'We consider them part of the cost of the tour. Would you like to browse in the gift shop before you leave?'

'Thanks, and yes. We'll browse.' Grey raised his eyebrows slightly and Soph nodded agreement.

'Is your foot up to it?' The farmer grinned. 'I can't drive the quadster into the store.'

Grey smiled back, a relaxed smile that said he had enjoyed his time here, that it had been worth it to organise the visit. 'I can manage a browse through a few shelves, I think.'

When the farmer nodded, Soph took Grey's arm and turned towards the interior of the building. In contrast to his apparent relaxation, tension coiled inside her. She dropped his arm after all. 'Great. Let's take a look, then.'

She could do this—take care of him in the role of employee and helper and nothing else. This could work. It *was working*. No reason why it shouldn't continue to do so all the way to the end of her contract with him.

They'd moved to a higher plane of existence now. At least she had. She had!

'I'll leave you both to look around.' Their farmer guide gestured them towards the interior of the shop.

'My sister will come over in a while to see if you want to buy anything.'

Soph left the dried flowers on the side table in the entry and they wandered through the place. There were more dried flowers and some mass-produced Australiana items—teaspoons with echidnas and possums on them, coat-hangers with handles made to look like kookaburras. Postcards and tea towels jostled for space with Styrofoam beer mug covers.

There were pottery vases too—beautiful things in all shapes and sizes and rich earth tones, both glazed and unglazed.

'Oh, they're made locally. See the sticker?' Soph turned one of the vases over to show Grey, holding it reverently because they were truly beautiful, carefully crafted with breathtaking floral designs.

He bent his head close to look, inhaled a long, slow breath and stepped back. 'Choose enough of them to display the wild flowers in the house and…pick one out for each of my stepmothers. They might like them.' On those words he turned away and focused his attention elsewhere in the small shop, but he turned back a moment later.

'Leanna might like that one.' He pointed to a vase. 'She had a painting once that reminded me of the design on the vase.'

He helped pick the other stepmothers' vases and Soph thought it was such a good thing that she felt all mushy inside until he said he hoped the sister would hurry up and get there because he'd had enough, and stomped his way to the far corner of the shop.

Grumpy Grey was back.

Soph caught herself inexplicably grinning, though the smile had an edge of sadness. She picked out small hand-crafted fridge magnets with floral designs for her sisters and forced herself to focus wholly on the task and not think about anything else.

The farmer and his sister stepped into the cottage together. Soph paid for her little purchases. Grey asked the woman to tally his up and, while she did so, sent Soph outside with the farmer to load the boxed items into the car.

'I'd thought of suggesting lunch.' Soph glanced at Grey as she slowed the car at the end of the farm road. What if he was tired? What if he'd had enough of her close company already? What if he guessed how much she had enjoyed being with him this morning?

She didn't usually second-guess herself or fill up with doubts, but they hammered at her now.

'There's a pub in the small township about ten kilometres from here.' If Grey caught her concerns, he ignored them. Instead he gestured to indicate the direction while his gaze lingered on her hair and then shifted away. 'Why stop the day now? Aren't we supposed to be entertaining ourselves?'

Oh, yes. Soph was vastly entertained by the direction of her thoughts and feelings, and her apparently complete inability to control them. She was so entertained she was about to implode as a result. She dipped her head and turned the car towards the pub, though.

After all, how much harder could she find it to be in his company for a meal out than for any other purpose at his house? In truth, it would probably be easier.

Soph's hands tightened on the wheel and she drew a deep breath.

Yes. This was sure to be heaps easier.

CHAPTER TEN

TO KEEP her whirling thoughts under control, Soph instigated a conversation about the farm—about flowers, vases, anything to fill the air with sound so she didn't think of anything else.

Grey let her talk, though he didn't contribute a whole lot to the conversation.

She pulled to a stop in a parking space in front of the pub with a sigh that was part relief and part no idea what to do with herself. A blue heeler dog sat on the welcome mat at the pub's front door, looking bored or possibly comatose. Soph reached for her door handle. 'I wonder if the dog is friendly.'

'Or even if it's conscious.' Grey added the mild words with a spark of something close to humour.

Something inside Soph's chest squeezed as she tried to smile in return. She forced her gaze away from Grey's face and looked up at the sky where fat cotton-wool clouds scudded along. The fear that she might be falling a little in love with him grew. Soph didn't want to fall. She couldn't afford to do that.

I'm not falling in love with him. I will protect myself from that.

She would fall in love when she was ready, with some bland, non-threatening man. Except the idea had lost all appeal. And she wasn't sure what she was afraid of any more—just that she did have fears in there somewhere.

'Let's brave the dog, anyway.' Grey pushed his door open and climbed out. 'We can eat and forget ourselves for a while.'

'That would be nice.' Soph didn't know if it was possible, but the idea had merit. She joined him and they moved towards the pub door. Their hands bumped lightly as they walked. Even that made her feel warm and sad and worried all at once.

'Do you think the dog wants us to believe it's a statue?' The dog's sides moved rhythmically and Soph had no doubt that it knew they were there, despite its stillness otherwise. Determined to pull herself out of this rattled state, she raised her voice slightly and pitched her words right at the canine doormat. 'Or maybe it expired there and nobody's noticed?'

The tail thumped up and down on the mat and Grey gave a soft chuckle. 'Look at that. It lives.'

They had to step over the hound. It didn't bite

them. Soph suspected this was a rite of passage for all who entered the pub.

Inside, there were two groups of old men at tables and a number of younger ones on stools, eating their lunches at the bar itself. As she and Grey stepped into the bar, every head turned. Someone gave a low whistle and, inexplicably, heat raced into her cheeks.

'Do you have a beer garden?' Grey had seen the blush. His gaze lingered on it for just a moment before he shifted it to the scribbled chalk board menu above the bar.

'There's a private room,' the bartender offered. 'It doesn't get used much for actual meals. It's at the back with a…ah…a view of the rear of the premises.'

'That will do.' Grey turned to Soph. 'What would you like from the menu? Battered fish? Roast of the day? Rissoles and veg?'

'I'd like a meat pie with chips and gravy, please, and…' she paused to think '…a glass of lemon squash.'

Grey nodded. 'I'll have the same, but with a light beer instead.' He paid for their meals.

The bartender pointed them towards the back of the pub. 'Just go through that door and then into the room on the left. The local craft ladies' guild uses the room three days a week, but not today.'

Once they were seated at one of half a dozen

square tables, Soph said, 'We could have eaten out there. I wouldn't have minded.'

'Maybe I didn't want to share you with twenty admirers,' he said grouchily and sighed. His mouth turned down at the corners and he glanced away.

Soph forced her attention to the view, what there was of it. The window was small and low in the wall. 'That's a nice view of…um…of scraggly grass and maybe half a broken-down wood shed?'

'Yes, very interestingly rustic.' His gaze came back to her and softened and he reached into his pocket and drew out a small wrapped package. 'This is for you. I spotted it at the farm's gift shop and…thought you might like to have it.'

Soph's heart did an odd little tripping thing. She took the small packet and unwrapped it. 'It's gorgeous.' She held the painted ceramic brooch in the palm of her hand and struggled with the desire to fling herself across the table at him and hold him so tightly he wouldn't be able to breathe.

Grey was watching her and, when her gaze lifted to his, her pleasure was reflected in his eyes.

She swallowed hard. 'The Waratah flower looks so real.' Red, bright, large, with prickly outer petals on the flower itself, the brooch would look great on a lapel or holding a scarf together, or in the middle of the brim of one of her crocheted hats in winter. 'Thank you, Grey. It was very thoughtful of you.'

'I'm pleased you like it.' He watched her pin it to the collar of her blouse and his gaze darkened and the air around them became loaded and breathless.

'I don't really have the right colours on, but I want to wear it straight away.' Her words wobbled just a little.

'Sophia—' He spoke her name in a deep, dark voice with not a speck of grouch or grumble to be heard in it.

'Two pies with chips and gravy as promised, with a healthy serving of veggies on the side because we're an equal opportunity food vendor.' The bartender laughed at his joke, plonked the plates on to the table, added their drinks and walked out again, whistling.

They turned their attention to their meals then, and talked about this and that as they ate their way slowly through the tasty, filling fare. Inside the room, it was intimate and cosy, the air so still somehow that Soph hardly dared to breathe and kept her voice to a quiet murmur.

When a ringing sound came from her tote bag she quickly drew Grey's cellphone out, looked at the caller ID and handed it to him. They'd agreed to carry the phone in case of emergencies and had instructed his company heads accordingly, but she'd forgotten she had it in there. 'Here's hoping there's not too much of a problem.'

'Let's find out.' Grey took the phone from Sophia.

He let his fingers touch hers as he did so, and then wondered if he was a fool. Couldn't he keep his hands to himself even through a single lunch? It appeared not.

She drew her hand away and touched the brooch with the tips of her fingers as she had done several times during the meal.

Her obvious pleasure fed his, and fed his need for her.

'Barlow.' He growled the word into the phone.

The caller was Peter Coates. Grey listened to him with half an ear and couldn't take his gaze from Sophia.

'...and they've committed to buy over half the apartments in the complex.' Coates's words finally penetrated and Grey straightened in his chair.

'Could you sum that all up again for me?' This time he listened carefully and surprise and pleasure built until he ended the call with thanks and congratulations and passed the phone back to Soph.

'What was it?' She tucked the phone away, but her gaze never left his face. 'Was it good news? You look sort of stunned but not upset.'

He picked one last chip off his plate and ate it while he let the news sink in.

'The Beacon's Cove project is back on track for the original completion date, and we've just had a consortium of buyers agree to purchase more than half of the apartments in the complex. We already have buyers for most of the rest. Coates and McCarty are to be congratulated. They've pulled off a real coup with this.'

'That's great news.' Her fingers almost reached across the table to his but, at the last moment, she dropped her hand into her lap instead. 'I'm so pleased, Grey. You've obviously got some talented and dedicated people working on your behalf.'

'I guess I do.' He fell silent. That didn't mean that he had to do anything differently. Not once he had the all-clear to get back in the thick of things.

And was that what he still wanted? That frenetic, sterile existence that allowed no room for feelings?

He paused and frowned.

It was.

Wasn't it?

He gestured towards her plate. 'Are you finished?'

'Yes.'

They got to their feet together and moved towards the door. He glanced at his watch and discovered they had lingered quite a long time over their meal.

As they stepped out of the pub, he realised just how much things had changed while they'd sat in the cosy haven and he'd taken notice of nothing but her. A storm front had rolled in.

Dark clouds hung low overhead. The dog had left his place on the mat to crouch beneath a bench against the wall of the pub, and the cars and utility vehicles belonging to the lunch crowd were all gone.

'I think we'd better get home.' Soph hurried to the car. 'I mean, back to the house.'

'Yes, we should hurry.' He climbed into the car, but his thoughts remained stuck on what she had said—*we'd better get home*.

It sounded close, intimate. He fell silent, his thoughts a jumble, all seeming to centre around Sophia. When he became aware of the storm again they were on the narrowest part of the road, winding mountainous terrain with barely room for two cars to pass.

Lightning forked once in a jagged arc, thunder boomed overhead and then, without further ado, the storm opened up right on top of them.

Soph flinched and her hands tightened on the wheel. 'The wipers can't keep up with this rain and the wind is rocking the car.'

'Try to stick to your lane. Keep the rough edge of the bitumen under the far side wheel but don't go off it.' He took care to speak in a calm, even tone and didn't point out the obvious. If she went off the road—really went off—he doubted the flimsy guard rails would stop them.

'That might be easier said than done.' She did it anyway, though.

Grey couldn't help the surge of pride in her that

filled him as she negotiated each treacherous kilometre of road. He wished he was the one behind the wheel so she didn't have to face the stress, but she was coping.

The car veered slightly on to the verge twice. Both times she steered it back on to the bitumen without jerking the wheel, her mouth tight, brown eyes wide and worried as she tried to see through those sheets of falling rain.

They got a break almost at the end of the worst of the mountain road. The wind died back for a while and the rain fell a little less heavily.

'Do I keep going or try to find somewhere to stop?' she asked with all of her concentration on the road.

'Can you keep going? The house isn't far now and the road is better here.' He hesitated. 'Only if you feel you can, Soph. Otherwise, we'll pull off and wait it out and get someone to tow us out if we get bogged.'

'I'll go on. I can do it.'

The wind had picked up again by the time they reached the house, and so had the heaviness of the rain. It hammered at the car from all sides in a deafening roar.

Soph drew the car to a stop within inches of the front steps. He wondered if she realised that she had almost nicked them with the passenger side wheels.

Her face was pale and strained now—sheet-white. Yet she turned to him and, though her voice shook and her hands shook, her first thought was for her job, watching out for him. She shouted over the rain, 'Can you take your shirt off and wrap it around your cast so it doesn't get soaked? Is there an umbrella in the car?'

'Yes to the first question and no to the second, unfortunately, but a little water won't hurt me.' He was more concerned about her, but she didn't give him time to say so.

Instead, she waited expectantly and Grey manoeuvred out of his pullover shirt in the confines of the car. He let her help him wrap it around his cast and then he cautioned her, 'Be careful on the steps. They're slate. They'll be slippery.' He wanted to tell her what a great job she had done, but maybe they should get inside first.

'I'd rather fall down the steps now we're safely here, than off the side of a mountain in your car.' Though she tried to make a joke of it, he heard the strain in her voice.

They made their way inside. Both got soaked in the process, though Grey's wrapping protected his cast. Once inside, they stood in the foyer while drips rolled off their bodies and clothing and they looked at each other. He peeled his shirt from his cast.

'You did great. You kept us both safe.' With a sigh, he tossed the shirt on the mat and reached out to wipe a dribble of green rain from the side of her face. Her hair was running and somehow the sight was both vulnerable and so much Sophia that it made his insides clench.

'I can't believe the deluge out there. I was terrified I'd get us both killed.' She made the confession, then lowered her gaze, trembling as she lost the fight with the control that had carried her through and the reality of what she had faced sank in.

'Come here, baby.' He pulled her against him, wet clothing, his bare chest, her runny hair and all. It felt good to hold her. Because of the storm and the danger they'd been in. Because he needed to and she needed it right now, as well. He indulged himself.

Breathed in her scent and kissed the top of her head and didn't care if he got green lips.

When her arms snaked around his middle awkwardly, trying to avoid his arm in its cast, Grey shoved both arms around and behind her so she could snuggle as close as could be.

That was what she did, and he caught his breath and fought not to crush her to him.

Maybe it was only the aftermath of her fear, but Grey wanted her there. He held her and patted her back through her sodden clothes and felt her shudder and finally press into him and the shudders leave her.

Their bodies warmed to each other and he became aware of every nuance of the way they fitted together—her breasts against his chest, the soft cradle of her tummy against his hips.

He would have kissed her, but she dropped her arms from around him and stepped back. 'I need to bring Alfie in from the shed and then change these clothes. You need to get dry too.' Her gaze roved over his chest and shifted back up to his face. 'It's chilled off so I suggest something warm.'

She hurried towards the laundry room door and escaped before Grey could speak a word.

Instead, he hobbled into the living room and turned on the heater so it could start to warm things and then headed upstairs to get into dry clothes. His arms still ached with the need to snatch her close and keep her close.

After that perilous drive to get them back here, his resistance to her was at zero, and he was damned if he could even make himself care.

But Soph seemed to have pulled herself together, to have overcome any inclination towards intimacy she may have felt.

Maybe she'd just needed a hug—anyone would have done.

Grey stomped into his bathroom. He was getting good at doing that and hobbling at the same time.

CHAPTER ELEVEN

IN A quite ferocious storm, it hammered relentless rain for the rest of the day. Soph tried to be cheerful and optimistic and most of all to keep her emotional distance from Grey.

She pretty much failed, but she hoped she kept that from him. Once they were both warm and dry and full of cardamom coffee, she left Alfie curled on the sofa in the living room, set up Grey's portable stereo system in the kitchen and spent the afternoon cooking to her favourite music CDs over the racket of the rain.

And in Grey's disturbing company. He helped her, chatted to her and in general, by his mere nearness, kept her awareness of him at a high.

Soph no longer had green hair. Since half the colour had washed away when she'd got soaked she'd taken a quick shower and got rid of the rest, letting her hair dry just any old how because she had no intention of trying to look beautiful for Grey.

Oh, no, she did not, and the choice of her absolute favourite blue jeans and her best fluffy rainbow jumper meant nothing anyway, so there.

They ate dinner to metal rock played by an obscure band. Retired to the living room and listened to reggae. Sipped hot chocolate to moody jazz and, when Soph felt her emotions were getting out of hand, she put on the soundtrack to one of her favourite G-rated, kid-oriented movies.

Rain rained, everything dripped and Grey sat silently in his chair and she sat silently on the sofa. Only Alfie the rabbit seemed content with his lot, curled beside her with his nose on his paws.

'I hope this weather doesn't cause problems. There are several creeks that come down out of the mountains that are already overflowing with snow melt.' Grey got to his feet, went to the window and peered out into the beating rain and darkness.

'I guess we'll have to wait and see.' Soph's heart beat in time with the rain as, now that Grey's back was turned, she let her gaze take in every inch of him. He looked better than wonderful in black trousers that moulded to strong thighs and a firm, appealing rear. His narrow waist widened into broad shoulders beneath a loose cotton long-sleeved shirt.

She had touched his skin, had hugged him tight and wanted so much more. There was no point in denying it. She wanted to make love with Grey, wanted that so much she couldn't seem to put it out of her mind. 'Um, what happens if the creeks overflow?'

'We could end up trapped here. It would be unusual, but the length and heaviness of this rain storm has been exceptional.' Grey swung away from the window. Their gazes locked and all of her thoughts and all of his desire locked for long moments as heat rushed through her.

His muscles tightened. Neck, face, body.

'Bed. That is, it's…um…I think I'll turn in.' She scooped up the rabbit. 'I'll just give Alfie a bit of fresh air first. There's a nice strip of grass that gets sheltered by the rear section of veranda.'

Her pet snuggled into her. He probably wouldn't like her half as much when she took him outside and dumped him on the grass, but Soph headed for the laundry room door anyway.

'I think I'll listen to music a while longer. Your CD collection intrigues me.' Grey kept his tone even, almost flat. Maybe he did like her music; in fact, he really seemed to, but was he keeping away from her too?

If he is, that's smart, and far more sensible than you seem to be right now.

'Then I'll just take care of Alfie's needs and I guess I'll see you in the morning.' Soph exited, stage Laundry Door, and let the cold, wet air outside soothe her overheated face as the rain continued to pelt down.

If only it would wash away her feelings for Grey at the same time.

'There's a problem upstairs—from the storm.' Sophia spoke the words from the living room doorway in an odd, disturbed tone. She still had the rabbit clutched in her arms. Indeed, she had only disappeared upstairs moments ago.

Grey had sat, refusing to think of her slowly removing those sprayed on jeans, lifting the fluffy jumper and revealing nakedness beneath, exposing the body that had teased and tantalised him all evening. She had curves to go with her full, lush lips. He wanted to explore all of them.

He forced his thoughts to her words. 'What's wrong?'

'We've lost power up there.' She stepped forward into the living room, set the rabbit down on the sofa and stood with her arms hugged around her middle. 'I flicked the light switch in my room and nothing happened. It's the same in all the rooms.'

'The house is on circuit breakers. I'll go outside and turn the switch back on—'

'Unfortunately, I don't think it's going to be that simple.' An edgy sound that was half laugh, half tension, escaped her. 'You see, it appears the roof has leaked…um…truckloads, actually, which is probably what put an end to the power up there. Do you have a torch?'

Grey came to his feet and moved close to her. 'There's a torch in the utility drawer in the kitchen. Let's hope the battery still works.'

Once he located the torch and tested it, he headed up the stairs.

She hadn't exaggerated the damage. Rain had come through the roof in Sophia's room, soaking the bed and carpet. The same had happened in the third bedroom, in one half of the landing and, to a lesser degree, in the bathroom she used.

His was the only upstairs room not affected. 'The water probably ran along the beams until it found places to come through the ceiling. It must have flowed away from my room rather than towards it.'

'The base of Alfie's basket got wet but it's made of sturdy cane so I don't think there'll be a problem. I've changed the piece of towel for a dry one.' Soph offered these words from outside the door of Grey's room.

While he had stepped inside to shine the torch around, she had hovered in the hallway. Now her concerns poured out. 'If I hadn't insisted on music all afternoon we might have heard what was happening.'

At that, Grey swung to face her. The torchlight cast her face in planes and shadows and worried angles. He joined her on the landing. 'We wouldn't have heard a few more drips above the racket of the storm going on outside. You're not responsible for any of this, Soph. I can replace the damaged items, get it all repaired.

'In truth, I should have had the roof checked out long ago. The electrician pointed out some wear and tear up there, but I never got around to engaging a tiler to have a look.'

She puffed up on his behalf. 'You couldn't have known there'd be a storm like this—'

'Exactly, and you couldn't have known the storm might make the roof leak.' Why did she feel such a compulsion to take responsibility? 'I think the question is—what do we do now?' Their options were limited. 'There's no point in trying to do anything about the leaks. Everything's soaked already. But meanwhile the bed in your room is out of commission. So is the one in the spare room. The sofa downstairs seats two at a pinch. Even curled up, neither of us would fit on it for the night.'

She drew a tight breath. 'I'll sleep sitting up on the sofa—'

Grey spoke at the same time. 'You can take the bed. I'll sleep on the floor—'

They both stopped.

Soph frowned at him. 'You can't sleep on a hard surface like that. It would be bad for your injuries.'

'And neither of us will get any sleep on that squashed up sofa.' He pointed it out and acknowledged that she was right—he wouldn't sleep well without the benefit of a decent mattress under him. Nor could he allow her to do that. 'Don't offer to take the floor. I'd stay awake all night feeling guilty.' But the alternative…?

'If I don't sleep on the floor or try to sleep on the sofa, and you mustn't either, we'll have to…share your bed.' She all but whispered it. The appalled look on her face as she absorbed this realisation gave his ego a bit of a beating until she glanced at the bed and back at him and he saw the confusion and uncertainty in her eyes. 'If you wouldn't mind letting me—'

'There's plenty of room for both of us.' *If he didn't mind letting her sleep beside him?* So close he could touch, yet he mustn't touch her. He wanted her so much his teeth ached. But it was the only viable alternative and she was halfway to accepting it.

He pushed her the rest of the way, gestured towards the bed and made himself say the words to reassure her. 'We need to sleep, and tomorrow we'll sort out what else we need to do.'

'We do need to sleep, don't we?' She chewed her lip.

'Why don't you go downstairs and turn off the

stereo and the heater? I'll get changed while you do that. You can bring your things and change in the bathroom, and then we'll go to sleep.' He tried for an encouraging smile. 'All right?'

'I—I guess so,' Soph answered Grey's question, wishing she didn't sound so uncertain. Sheesh, she wasn't some dubious virgin from a bygone era who didn't know what went on in the bedroom, or how to make her own choices on the subject.

No, she was just a dubious virgin from this era who knew exactly what could go on and wanted it too much for her own comfort.

She pinched her lips together. So she had never trusted a man enough to give him that much of herself. What of it?

'I'll be back in ten minutes, if that's long enough?' When he nodded, Soph swung around and hurried away. She carried pans upstairs and scattered them about to try to catch drips. And then she made up jobs to keep her downstairs longer than the ten minutes. Maybe Grey would have dozed off by the time she returned to his room.

To share his bed for the night.

Just the two of them.

Not even Alfie would be in the room because, well, she couldn't expect Grey to want a rabbit in a basket beside him. He'd been tolerant enough of Alfie, but not exactly…enamoured. Instead, she trudged up the stairs and settled her pet in his basket in a dry corner of the corridor.

Completely procrastinating now, she fussed some more to ensure the rabbit's comfort, not that he seemed to care. He was blobbed out and almost asleep already. Then, because she couldn't delay any longer, Soph gathered her pyjamas and toothbrush from her room and the bathroom—thank goodness her clothes had stayed dry in the cupboard—and stepped quietly into her boss's bedroom.

And there was Grey.

In the bed.

Naked. The top half of him, at any rate. Naturally, he wouldn't be naked beneath the sheets, or she certainly hoped not! Soph realised she had come to a standstill to stare, and Grey stared right back at her, his eyes managing to look both somnolent and sharply interested in the candlelight.

'You brought the aromatherapy candle from your bathroom.' The one she had placed there. She edged towards his *en suite* bathroom with the torch in her free hand. 'It…um…it smells great and thank you for thinking of some light for us. We should probably conserve the torch battery, I guess. I'll be as quick as I can.'

Soph clutched her pyjamas and toothbrush tighter against her chest and dashed into the bathroom. 'Don't stay awake on my account, though. You're probably exhausted and want to go to sleep this instant.'

She slapped the bathroom door shut behind her and leaned against it. With her eyes closed, she wondered what other inane things she could have said. After a moment, the cold of the room began to penetrate and Soph reluctantly moved forward to clean her teeth and get ready for bed. They really did have to conserve the torch battery.

She could do this. It was no big deal. He probably didn't think it was a big deal. He'd probably had plenty of women share his bed. Hmph. Soph helped herself to some of Grey's mouthwash and gargled loudly.

Finally there was nothing else to do, no other means to put off the inevitable. She opened the bathroom door a crack, slipped through it, turned off the torch and put it on the floor where she would be able to reach it and, without looking at Grey once, slid beneath the covers and curled up into a ball at the edge of the bed.

Grey shifted and sighed on his side of the bed—obviously not asleep.

Soph realised, belatedly, that she hadn't helped him with his ankle exercises before they'd turned in. 'Your physio—are you uncomfortable?'

'Yes, I am quite uncomfortable.' He muttered the words in a low tone that rushed her senses and made her blush in the darkness. 'The ankle doesn't feel great either, but I'm sure I'll survive. Go to sleep, Sophia.'

'Grey—?' She stopped because she didn't know what she wanted to say to him, and there wasn't anything really, was there? Not that could be said. Not that she *should* say. 'Goodnight.'

'Goodnight.' He rolled away from her in the dim light, so his back was turned. The scent of the candle wafted in the air, but it wasn't a patch on the scent of warm man—of Grey—beside her.

She was in his bed, for heaven's sake. Well, she had better just put that thought aside and get some rest. Thank goodness Grey had some control, because otherwise she would be right over there getting as snug as possible with him.

Yes, thank goodness for Grey's control. It had turned out to be a good thing after all, hadn't it? She let out a long, disgusted sigh and buried her face in her pillow.

When that didn't seem to help, she flipped over on to her back, and then her other side, and, after some more shuffling about, finally settled in to begin the long and strenuous journey towards insensibility.

Surely, sooner or later, she would manage to fall asleep? When she woke it would be morning, she would have survived this night of being close to Grey and not letting herself touch him or snuggle into him or do any of the other things she so desperately wanted to do with him.

They would get up and be boss and employee again, and they would find out how to fix the roof and replace everything—he was right.

It wasn't her responsibility, so why did she feel she needed to contribute and couldn't?

Soph shifted positions again, seeking that comfortable place that wasn't to be found either mentally, physically or emotionally.

Tomorrow would be better. It had to be. She drifted into a restless sleep.

Grey wanted Sophia. His body ached from his toenails to the ends of his hair, but he was keeping to himself—just. She'd wiggled and sighed and buried her face in his pillow and squirmed and shifted and wiggled some more until finally, after what felt like at least two hours, she'd drifted into a genuine sleep.

Only then did Grey relax enough to release his breath in a long sigh of his own, and he rolled towards her. Damned if he didn't. He pulled his pillow closer to hers and ignored the twitchy feeling in the leg with the damaged ankle attached, and instead buried his face close to her hair.

It was heaven and hell, but eventually the room and the scent of the candle and the hours he had been awake enabled him to find his way towards slumber, despite the tight coil of his body, the need.

His feelings for Sophia were deepening. Grey grimaced as he wearily acknowledged that. He wanted her in more ways than a mere physical joining. He wanted to understand what made her tick, wanted to see inside her soul. Grey had never wanted that with another woman, had thought himself incapable of such things, to be truthful.

If he let it happen he could fall for her…but he couldn't. He didn't want to open the same can of worms his father had exposed him to through all his marriages. The fights and emotional upheaval and each of his stepmothers eventually leaving. He didn't blame Leanna or Dawn or Sharon—his father had hurt each of them. Grey had never felt particularly close to him either, and he'd struggled because of his father's actions. He didn't want that turmoil in his adult life.

Sophia made a snuffling sound in her sleep, flipped over and burrowed her nose against his neck, where she proceeded to snore softly.

A well of tenderness rose up and threatened to engulf him. Grey's chest ached—not with pain and not because of stress—but because of Sophia. His body knitted itself to hers—angles to curves, hard to soft—even though he had lots of noble reasons not to touch her. It felt right. He sighed against her hair and left his mouth there, where he could feel her warmth through his lips, inhale her scent and enjoy her nearness.

He would move away before morning. She didn't need to know how she had tempted him. Finally, he too slept.

'Argh!' Grey's sound of pain jolted Soph from a warm, bone-melting sleep to wakefulness quickly enough for her to feel him draw away from her, realise they had been curled in each other's arms, and then understand his distress as he sat up in the bed, shoved his pyjama leg unceremoniously up and wrapped his fingers around his calf.

'You've got a cramp.' She came to her knees in the bed and tossed the covers out of the way. 'Let me.'

Her words were sleep-slurred. So was her vision. Soph ignored those things and massaged his clenched muscles. For minutes he reclined back on one elbow, teeth gritted, while she worked the knots out for him.

Gradually, as the muscles relaxed under her ministrations, Soph became aware of other things. The chill of the room against her bare arms. Grey's leg beneath her fingers, hairy and masculine and warm. The candle that still burned, adding its mellow aroma to the room. And Grey's scent, mingled with hers, of warm sheets and close bodies and nighttime and desire.

Her hands stopped moving. He sat up at the same time and their gazes locked. There was no rain outside now. No sound but that of their breathing in the stillness of the room, nothing for Soph to see but the heat and the questions in his eyes.

Confusion, desire, hunger and need, all shone there for her to see. His gaze dipped to her mouth, rose back to lock on her eyes. His fingers circled her wrist. No other part of their bodies touched. Yet fire sliced through her, a hot burn that made her fears insignificant, her uncertainties a mere foolish blockade that stopped her from being in his arms, from having the chance to make love with him.

So what if it was only tonight? Why couldn't they take that and let it go in the morning? Lots of people did that. *Grey* had almost certainly done that, though she didn't want to think of him in another woman's arms.

'I want what's in your eyes. I want you to make it real, Grey, right now, tonight.'

He froze for a moment and then said in a tone that was almost menacing, 'Do you understand what you're saying?'

But she knew all his grouches and growls now, knew they didn't mean a thing, not really. 'I know.'

'Dear God, I can't not do this. Not when you look at me that way.' He pulled her against him, swept her against his body, back on to the pillows, as he kissed her and kissed her.

Ravishing, plundering kisses and soft worshipful ones until she was breathless and desperate, her hands everywhere, touching him, revelling in him as he seemed to revel in her.

Then he started all over, so gentle with her as he learned her curves and encouraged her to learn him too. His body was hard, his touch so tender. He pressed kisses to her face and her neck and her eyelids; propping himself half over her, he stroked her face, shaped the curve of her shoulder. Finally, he cupped one breast and then the other through the soft material of her sleeveless top.

He curved his hand down, over the indent of her waist, over the soft rise of her belly. His gaze never left hers and his eyes told her he liked her body, found her attractive.

This was Grey and she wanted him to want her. More than she had cared what any other person thought of her in any way there was.

'I want to touch you, Sophia, skin to skin,' he murmured and hot and cold shivers filled her, and then his hand was there again and her top was gone. Her heart raced as tension and need built inside her at each touch of his hand, each deep, drugging kiss.

Soph touched him too—touched him everywhere

she wanted to touch—until finally there was no clothing any more and he prepared himself. She wondered about his plaster cast and his ankle and whispered her worry out loud, 'How…?'

'Don't worry about how.' He kissed her again, moving her until they lay facing each other. He shifted so they could fit together and, as he pushed forward, the barrier in her body yielded to take him in.

'Soph.' The word was agonised. He stopped very still and swallowed hard. 'Oh, God, Sophia.' He kissed her then, and his mouth trembled over hers.

'It doesn't hurt.' Not as much now. She knew it would ease—it already was. 'Please, don't stop.' She held him fiercely and, after a moment, she whispered, 'Love me, Grey. Love me as much as you can.'

CHAPTER TWELVE

GREY'S heart thundered in his chest. Emotion threatened his control as he drew Sophia even closer against him. His throat worked as he held her, stroked her back, wondered what he had done to deserve this moment, this gift. He didn't deserve it, but Soph had given it to him anyway.

He blinked his eyes hard and dropped a kiss on her parted lips, praying she couldn't see.

'I can't…' *Find the words for what I feel, can't tell you.* He dipped his head and tried to show her. Kissed her mouth, felt that brush of her lashes against his cheek that he had imagined, and now knew he had longed for.

She smiled—a soft, sweet parting of her lips—and her face softened and relaxed as her body adjusted to his presence.

He loved her then, just as she had asked, as much as he could. Their gazes locked together and he thought he could stay this way for ever, her arms twined around his back, her soft skin everywhere against him.

Each breath she took made him shudder with need. He held back his completion until she arched, his name a cry on her lips. He fell with her then, fell into satiation, fell with feelings he had never experienced before and couldn't comprehend, even now. He could only feel them, their depth and their strength, and acknowledge they were tied up in her.

She sighed and wrapped her arms around him, all the way around his waist, and hugged up close against him.

Grey stroked his fingers through her hair and let the silky-soft texture play over his skin. The thought of tomorrow pushed forward. He pushed it back and knew he wanted her now more than ever.

'You were beautiful.' The emotion rose again. Soph had unmanned him with her generosity and her innocence and her openness. 'I wish I hadn't hurt you.'

I wish I would never hurt you again.

'You made me forget soon enough.' Her eyelids fluttered half-closed as her words began to slur. 'I think I'd like to snuggle with you now. You're probably better than a hot-water bottle. I've always thought you would be…so warm…'

Grey bit back an unexpected overwrought laugh.

The words had only just left her when her lashes fluttered one final time and she went under.

'I want to hold you while you sleep.' He whispered this truth as he slipped from the bed and padded into the bathroom. He thought she might wake when he joined her again, but she didn't.

With a deep sigh, he shifted close, drew her head to his chest and tucked her body into the shelter of his own.

Now that he had made love with Soph, instead of feeling assuaged, he wanted something more with her. Grey didn't understand what that something was, or how to get it, or even if he could get it.

All he knew was he didn't want to let this end now. He wanted her in his arms, under him, her body his to love and know and cherish over and over.

Until?

Until it finished, he supposed.

Until they parted company when she finished working for him?

His arm tightened around her and his mouth firmed. With Soph locked against him and his thoughts locked against letting her go, he slept.

When the candle had burned out and the night was so dark and all Soph could do was feel, Grey woke her and made love to her again. She fell into the experience before she had time to think and then she couldn't have stopped if she tried.

He worshipped every inch of her, made her feel

treasured and glorious and powerful. Then that feeling of power fell away as her need for him took over. He shook in her arms too, whispered broken words to her as they tumbled over the brink a second time.

He fell asleep stroking her hair, but Soph didn't sleep straight away. Her thoughts wouldn't let her. Tonight she had done a monumental thing. She couldn't go back from it. She couldn't regret it either. Being with Grey this way felt right. Soph had given him a part of her heart tonight. She couldn't deny that.

Now she had to work out what to do, but with Grey's deep-seated need to avoid emotional entanglement, where could this go? She ignored any thoughts that she might need to examine her own attitudes and thinking. Grey didn't want commitment. That was a fact.

Chilled suddenly, Soph retrieved her nightclothes and put them on, and then drew the quilt over the bed.

'You don't have to say a thing.' Soph took a covert glance at Grey, where he sat up in the bed with his breakfast on a plate on his knees. It was morning and before she'd woken him she had slipped away to prepare their meal. She had worked out what she needed to say, had determined how she would go about saying it. But now that the moment was here, her courage wanted to desert her.

They had shared so much last night. She hadn't understood how that sharing would make her feel. How *much* she would feel, how it would stir longings in her, make her want things…

Soph didn't want to examine those longings in detail. Suffice it to place them under the general label of risking too much of an attachment to Grey if she let last night's intimacy continue. She had a job to do here. When it ended she would leave and help the next person the agency found for her. A certain level of emotional distance had to be maintained. And making love with Grey last night… Well, it hadn't been good for that distance.

She had to make her attitude clear. It was for the best.

So get on with it!

'I know you must agree with me.' In truth, she had no idea of Grey's thoughts. They were side by side in his bed. He had cardamom coffee clasped in one hand and a half-eaten plate of eggs on his lap. His jaw was like granite and his eyes a very bright, sharp green.

With his hair rumpled and the muscles of his chest and shoulders so beautifully displayed, he looked like every woman's fantasy. Soph just wasn't sure what mood the fantasy was in.

'We'll carry on as before and that will be fine, more than fine. I have no expectations here.' She stopped to tug uneasily at her pyjama top. 'I want to thank you for…last night. It…well…it satisfied our mutual curiosity.'

'I think it addressed more than a little inquisitiveness.' The frown between his brows deepened and, somehow, without appearing to do anything but stare at her, he made her tingle all over with remembered heat.

Soph forced herself to eat a bite of egg from her plate and took care not to let the fork clatter as she put it down again. 'Yes, well…um…that's right but it was sort of spur of the moment, wasn't it?' She took a sip of her coffee.

'Yes. That's not the point.' Grey set aside his coffee and jabbed his fork into a lump of egg.

She supplied helpfully, 'I flavoured the eggs with maple syrup and orange marmalade and chunks of dill pickles. I hope you like the taste.'

'The eggs taste just fine.' He jabbed some more on to his fork and chewed.

'Please don't be offended.' She offered the words in a voice that bordered on timid and forced herself to speak in a louder tone as she went on. 'You would have said the same thing this morning. I just happened to say it first.'

'How can you possibly know what I would have said?' He looked as though he wanted to turn his face to the ceiling and snarl until the roof caved in.

He couldn't be that upset, though, not really. 'I

know because you've made it clear you don't want any entanglements. We have a working relationship. That needs to be preserved and, with that in mind, it's best if last night doesn't happen again.'

'So you've decided to end it here and now.' He said it in such a mild tone, but his gaze burned through her.

'Well, yes, but *we've* decided. We're just agreeing about something, we're both being adult about it.'

Did he think her odd for tackling it this way, curled up in his bed, eating breakfast she had prepared before he could wake? She hadn't wanted to make a big deal of it, had wanted to seem sophisticated and in control of it all. But now she had reached her limits, felt the edge of despair trying to pull her down because a part of her didn't want him to agree, didn't want to stop this here.

'You're right, Sophia.' His fingers tightened around the mug he held. 'You're completely right. This does need to end here and now. It's best.'

'Well, that's good. I knew we could come to an agreement about it. Now, I think I've had enough breakfast.' She slipped from the bed, away from him, as she made the excuse. Away from the need to curl into a desperate lump in the bed and cry her eyes out. He'd capitulated. That was what she *wanted.* 'It's time I tended to Alfie, anyway. He seemed content in his basket when I checked but he probably wants to be taken outside by now, and you'll want a bath.'

They had shared so much, and she had realised too late that one taste of Grey—one week, one month, however long he might have kept her with him—could never be enough. That was the real fact, and Soph had managed this so-called 'calm and sophisticated' discussion about it with very little control to spare.

That control threatened to abandon her completely now. 'I'll get rid of the dishes and take care of Alfie and find some fresh clothes from my room and take a shower in the other bathroom. I can cope with a bit of water damage in there.'

It was the damage to her heart that was the problem now. Just as well she had only let herself love him a little. She backed out of the room.

Grey cursed his way through bathing and dressing. Fortunately, the water heating system was on a downstairs circuit, though a cold shower might have been a good idea. He went downstairs. The one reasonably good thing about this morning was that Soph hadn't said that she wanted to leave him completely, though he had no idea how he would cope with her small touches and kindnesses without reaching for her. It was a hell of a tangle, and he'd let it get this way. He could have restrained himself last night.

And missed the chance to hold her, possess her?

No. He wasn't sure he could have held back from that, not when she had been with him every step of the way.

Yet she was right. Deep inside, he knew it. It *was* better to stop this now, before either of them started to look for impossible things.

A helicopter arrived while he was on the phone, talking to the local authorities, finding out the extent of the flooding, which, as it turned out, was comprehensive. The worst this area had seen in a hundred years, with three separate bodies of water flooded across the main exit points in all directions.

Grey watched the helicopter land in the field near the house. Leanna and the pilot climbed out. His stepmother, incongruously, had gumboots on with what from this distance Grey guessed was probably a Chanel suit, complete with fancy hat. At another time he might have smiled at the sight. Instead, he watched her slosh across the waterlogged paddock towards the house and spoke quietly into the phone.

'No need to worry about us.' No need for him to share his bed with Sophia again tonight. No need to sleep with her scent close to him, to listen to the sigh of her breath and feel her warmth at his side. 'It appears the cavalry has arrived to execute an evacuation.'

He ended the call and met Sophia's gaze across the width of the living room. They'd done that since they'd discovered they were flooded in. Since he'd emerged from his room and found her in the kitchen, dressed in a deep red skirt and blouse with her hair gelled up in spikes. She had proceeded to act as though last night hadn't happened or, at the least, hadn't changed their working relationship.

They'd looked across rooms at each other and taken care not to get close. His arms hurt. His chest felt tight. As though, if he held her, it would all go away.

'The cavalry in the form of what?' Soph asked.

His stepmother answered Sophia's question for him.

'Yoo-hoo! Is anybody home?' she called and rapped smartly on the outer door. Grey moved forward to open it.

Leanna immediately wrapped him in a hug. 'We were all so worried when we heard about the terrible storm in this region.' She squeezed him and stepped back. 'Naturally, we investigated further. When we realised you wouldn't be able to get out, we organised transport. Since I'll be paying the largest portion for the helicopter hire, I got to be the one to come and see you safely back to Melbourne.' She looked concerned and relieved to find him in one piece.

'I'll cover the costs of the helicopter.' Had he been so tough when they'd talked about money that they'd all felt they had to do this? He hadn't meant to be. 'I would have needed to organise something anyway.'

'I don't think you should pay, Grey dearest. The helicopter wasn't your idea.' She seemed discomfited but determined, and glanced over her shoulder. 'Let me introduce our pilot, anyway. I think he wants to talk to you about the need to move on quite quickly.'

Introductions duly made, the pilot, a competent-looking man in his fifties, dipped his head. 'It'd be best if we could leave within the next half hour. The weather is looking to close in again and I don't want to still be here when that happens.'

'Then we'll pack.' The time passed in a blur as they gathered their belongings and closed the house up as safely as they could and hustled to the helicopter.

Grey carried a travel bag on his shoulder and one in his hand, and hobbled along on a foot wrapped in three layers of plastic bags because Soph thought getting it cold and wet might be harmful to the sprain. He didn't give a damn, but he hadn't wanted to argue with her.

It was only as they settled into their seats that he let himself look at Soph and saw that her nerves were stretched tight. They'd brought Alfie along, of course, and Soph had him clutched in her arms. She and the rabbit both looked miserable.

'Give him to me.' He helped himself without waiting for Soph to agree and steeled himself not to react as their hands touched in the exchange. 'I'll tuck him against my jumper. It might feel a bit more secure for him.'

'Thank you.' She looked ready to cry and Grey's heart clenched at the knowledge.

He settled the rabbit. It was kind of comfy to hold, really, in a blobby-scared-fur-ball sort of way. He hoped it wouldn't choose now to break its house-trained record.

Leanna glanced at them once, and then turned her gaze to the scenery outside.

Soph clutched her hands together until the knuckles showed white against her skin. With the rabbit now settled, Grey eased one of her hands into his and held on when she would have drawn it away.

'We'll be in Melbourne before you know it. In the meantime, you're quite safe, truly.' He wasn't sure if he was, though, and forced himself not to tighten his grip against the moment when he would have to give up her hand.

'I'm not afraid.' Her chin was up and she looked determined to face anything. He wondered how often she faced the world like this and pretended she was fine when she wasn't.

He stared out of the window and watched Melbourne materialise beneath them. Couldn't he find a way to be with her without risking the kind of emotional fallout his father had brought on in all his relationships?

What sort of question was that, anyway? He would hurt her. That was the only outcome, no matter what he tried. Did he want that?

Before he could think himself into any greater pit of trouble, the helicopter landed. Leanna had her car waiting, and a hired one to see them back to Grey's apartment.

'No stress, Grey. We just wanted to get you safely out of there and now we'll let you get back to resting.' She disappeared before he could properly thank her.

The car took them to his town house. When they arrived Soph fussed over Alfie and settled him in his cage out the back. Grey watched from a distance and decided the rabbit looked as profoundly grateful to be on terra firma again as it was possible for a rabbit to be.

'You were kind to Alfie during the flight.' Soph spoke the words with a soft gleam in her eyes as she came back into the house. 'And you were kind to me. I've never been in a helicopter before. I was a bit concerned it might make me sick and I didn't want to be a nuisance or cause anyone any bother. I'm supposed to take care of you.'

'You're doing fine at that.' He simply now wanted

more from her. The thought of sharing his home with her and not being able to touch her, hold her, was impossible, yet that was how it would have to be.

'We're both without a car for now, but I should make a list and pick up some groceries.' Her gaze slid away from his. 'I can do that while you make the calls to arrange to have your country house repaired once people can get to it. I'll take a taxi.'

She made good on her word, and he let her, and he made his phone calls.

'Your country home is great, but I must admit it's nice to be back in the city too.' Soph had slipped into the house and unpacked the groceries while he finished up on the phone. She made the comment now as she started to help him with his physio. Talking to take her mind off their closeness?

She went on. 'How's the ankle feeling?'

'Better.' His injuries were improving. He hoped the doctor would confirm the same about his stress levels, though he didn't want to look ahead to the day that her work here would be over. 'You've had no time off since we started. I'd like you to see your sisters, go shopping.'

Do things that make you happy and then come back to me because, even though I know I don't make you happy, I can't completely let you go.

'I'd like to see them.' She bent and replaced and laced the ankle brace with deft, sure movements.

When she straightened, she nodded. 'I'll make plans. Does it matter when I take the time?'

'Whenever suits you.'

'I'll keep you occupied while we're here.' So committed to her job, despite all that had happened. 'You'll have to do your part by avoiding office stuff, including online business courses! But there are lots of things we can do. A matinee movie, the theatre, a trip up the Yarra River…'

Things that at another time could have been special, romantic. Yet he knew he would remember them, anyway.

'I haven't been to the movies in ages.'

They went to a shoot 'em up, knock 'em down movie. There, in the darkness, Soph seemed determined to shed the stresses that lay between them. She laughed when the bad guys got foiled, held her breath and let out little screams in the scary bits. Clutched his arm as the movie came to its finale.

But she let go before the lights went up.

Grey remembered it now as he stretched his legs out in front of him. They'd done all manner of things and this morning they were on the sun deck of a cruise boat. He hadn't seen Melbourne from the water like this for years, had forgotten the sight of the gardens and familiar landmarks. A pity the trip had to end so quickly. He sighed as the dock came into view again.

'That was wonderful, wasn't it? Peaceful and full of life all at once.' Soph leaned down to pull her bag from beneath her feet. The curve of her back and shoulders seemed so vulnerable beneath the turquoise cotton shirt. How would he survive without her brightness?

He stood and moved to the railing. Gripped it so he wouldn't reach for her. Since they'd returned to the city, they'd lived in a kind of nowhere land. They did things together. Sometimes he thought they both wanted to soak in the presence of the other without acknowledging the need.

Did Soph feel that way? He just knew he did and, though he cherished her company, he was also struggling with increasingly taut emotions because of that company, because he no longer knew what he wanted from her, *with her*. Even that thought wasn't exactly right. He wanted Sophia. That was simple enough. But he didn't know how he could have what he wanted.

He'd got tickets to the theatre for that night. Soph visited her sisters in the afternoon and came home with a dressmaker's bag in her hand. They ordered in a restaurant meal again and then she disappeared into her room to change clothes.

Grey wore evening trousers with a loose-fitting black shirt. He chose the outfit because he could put it on without help.

When Sophia emerged from her room, he glanced up as he rose from his seat on the sofa. 'You're ready? The taxi should be here any—' The rest of the words stopped in his throat. 'My God, that's… you're…' He lifted one hand towards her, dropped it back to his side and his fingers slowly curled as he took in the picture she made.

Her dress was a midnight-blue ankle-length sheath, bare on one shoulder with a wide ruffled band holding it on to the other. It cupped every curve and flared at her ankles. Bare toes painted red peeped from five-inch stiletto heels. She carried a wispy spider web shawl of silver lace and had curled her hair into waves that caressed her face and drew attention to her soft, generous mouth. Chandelier earrings brushed her neck as she moved her head.

'You look incredible, Sophia.' How would he keep his hands off her? It was difficult enough at any time.

Her smile was tentative, cautious, but pleasure lurked in the depths of her eyes. 'Thank you. Bella designed the gown for me. She's so successful now. Once, we used to all dress in her creations and go to the theatre and pretend we were posh superstars out for a night on the town. That was when she sewed on a machine in a corner of her room at the flat.'

A horn sounded outside. Grey wasn't sure whether to be pleased or disappointed. It was probably best to get out of the seclusion of the town house. 'I wish I'd had a car and driver for tonight so you could arrive in appropriate style.'

She laughed. 'I'm still just the girl employed by the We Work for You agency to help you out for a while. A taxi is perfectly appropriate, at least until our cars are returned to us when the flooding at your country house recedes.'

He wasn't convinced, but he let it go. When she curled the shawl around her shoulders and moved towards the door, he couldn't have spoken anyway. The dress wasn't immodest. It left only that one shoulder bare and a hint of back on the same side. Her shawl covered even that much, but he found even the slightest glimpse of her skin affected him. Her back was soft and feminine. Her shoulder gently sloped where it met her arm.

He wanted to strip her bare and just look at her, look at every beautiful inch.

'Grey? Is everything all right? Are you ready to go?' She stood with the door held open and looked over her shoulder at him.

'Yes.' *No, I'm not ready.* 'Yes, let's go.'

The performance was probably faultless. Grey couldn't have said because ninety-nine and a half per cent of his attention was focused on Sophia where she sat beside him. The evening was torturous and interminable because of that nearness and over too soon because he didn't want it to end.

'Perhaps a drink…' He made the suggestion as they emerged on to the street. Others crowded around them and Soph had a frown on her face and her elbows out like a mother hen determined to keep people away from him.

Something inside him melted. He hadn't anticipated it and couldn't have stopped it; it had simply happened.

'Nobody's going to hurt me, Soph, but I appreciate you wanting to stop it anyway.' He took her arm and tugged her away, the only thought in his mind to get her alone so he could kiss her.

'Your ankle—and your arm.' She was a little incoherent.

He wanted to make her a whole lot more so. 'Forget the drink. Let's go home.' The words rasped out. 'I want you where the world can't see us and I'm going to strip that beautiful dress from you an inch at a time…'

'You can't do that. We agreed—' She looked trapped and terrified and hungry for him all at once. But her hand rose and she laid her fingers over the sleeve of his shirt and the look in her eyes reflected the frustration and desire that must be shining from his own.

'Sophia.' Grey stepped forward to close the distance between their bodies, even the crowd around them now forgotten as he growled out her name.

'Grey? How—how lovely to see you out tonight.' The words came from his stepmother as she drew to an abrupt halt almost on top of them. 'I didn't realise it was you at first.' Leanna's face lit up for a moment before her smile slowly faded and uncertainty replaced it. Her gaze moved from him to Soph and back again and she stammered, 'I'm sorry. I've interrupted your evening. I'm with friends, anyway. It was a little stuffy inside and I came out ahead of them. I'll go back.'

'It's lovely to see you again, Leanna.' It was Soph who spoke, who stopped his stepmother's headlong flight away from them. 'You haven't interrupted anything. We were about to flag down a taxi and leave, that's all.' She drew a breath and, without catching Grey's eye, went on. 'It's been a long day and it's time to end it now.'

Grey's brows snapped down. She had dropped her hand away from him. It slowly dawned on him that he had lost all control in her presence yet again, this time in front of a hundred witnesses. And that she had saved him from that lack of control.

Leanna chewed her lip before she spoke to Grey again. 'You really didn't have to pay for that helicopter. We had it covered.'

'I know.' He looked past his frustration and into Leanna's eyes. He took her hand in his for the first time since he was a child and squeezed. 'How are you spending your days, Leanna? Are you happy? Enjoying life? I know you loved my father, but maybe there'll be someone else.'

Her eyes filmed with moisture and she blinked rapidly to dispel it. 'We all loved him, all three of us. People might think it's odd that we're now good friends, but somehow we turned to each other.

'I wish we could have drawn you in too, but you were so determined to keep everyone out and each time he left one of us…we let the hurt cloud our eyes and didn't see you needed us.' His stepmother drew a shaky breath. 'I regret that I let you down, Grey. I truly am sorry for that.'

Soph's hand gripped his arm again. This time Grey knew it was because she felt Leanna's emotion, felt sad for her.

And he acknowledged his part of the blame in the only way he knew how. 'I had my share of prickles out. Maybe we could try to change things.'

'All of us? Sharon and Dawn—'

'Yeah, all of us.' He cleared his throat.

Leanna smiled and some of the old sparkle came back to her eyes. 'Thank you, Grey. I think I can speak for all of us when I say we'll welcome any involvement you might like to have.'

His stepmother melted into the crowd while Grey was still battling with a suddenly tight throat. When he turned back to Soph her eyes were soft.

Her mouth trembled when she tried to smile at

him. 'I knew they loved you. I knew it right from the start, and I knew you loved them.'

Grey nodded acknowledgement because he couldn't really say anything. But it pleased him. It did. He felt hope for the future with his stepmothers, gratitude for the chance to try again and maybe manage to forge some kind of bond with each of them.

But it wouldn't be like that with Sophia. As far as that relationship was concerned, nothing had truly changed or would change. She was still light and laughter and happiness, and he would still take all that from her because he would inevitably let her go. He didn't know how to do anything else.

'I'll be glad when I'm rid of my physical impediments.' His frustration rang in his words. 'I need to get back to work.' He needed to take control of his life again.

She moved towards the kerb as a taxi cruised towards them from down the street. 'And when you're better I'll move on to my next assignment, the next person I can help.'

The taxi stopped at her hail. She let Grey open the rear door for her and climbed inside, waiting for him to join her and give the address to the driver.

Grey did so and refused to look at the vulnerable line of her back, the tensed shoulders.

Or to think how few days he had left with her.

CHAPTER THIRTEEN

SOPH couldn't do this any more. She climbed out of her bed in Grey's guest room at his town house the next morning with the conviction absolute in her mind.

She dressed and prepared him a healthy breakfast. When he came into the kitchen, she smiled and gestured him to a chair and bent to put the brace on as she had done so many times before.

It didn't matter if her smile felt strained and every touch or gesture or expression made her heart ache. She had a job to do.

'I popped out and bought the papers from the corner store so you can do the crossword puzzles and read the news and business pages.' She stepped away from him and brought the Welsh rarebit and frothed nutmeg milk drinks to the table.

He waited until she was seated before he spoke. 'I appreciate that. I'll look at them later. I'm going out this morning; I have follow-up appointments with Doc Cooper and the physio.'

'Oh, then I'll—'

'Leanna's going to drive me.' He dropped his gaze to his food. 'I rang her this morning and mentioned it and she offered.'

'That's great.' Soph chewed a piece of the toast and forced herself to swallow it. Her throat had tightened and she had to clear it before she spoke again. 'I'll find something to do, then. Actually, I'll stock your freezer with some meals for…for after I'm gone.' She barely stumbled as she said it.

He lifted his gaze but she couldn't read his thoughts. 'You'll have plenty of time to work undisturbed,' was all he said. 'I don't expect to be back until mid-afternoon.'

Soph nodded and they continued the meal in silence until Grey excused himself to finish getting ready.

When a horn tooted outside, he glanced back at her once as he stepped through the front door. His face was unsmiling, his green eyes turbulent.

It was as the door closed that Soph acknowledged that she had fallen utterly and completely and hopelessly in love with him. She had loved Grey the night of the rain storm—had probably loved him before that—loved his growl speak and his irritation and his stubborn struggle because he didn't want to cede control to others.

Grey was still fighting that battle. His doctor's appointment might end in fireworks again this morning. This time she wouldn't know unless he chose to say something about it, but she was glad that he wanted to let his stepmothers back into his life. Soph sniffed hard and went into the kitchen and dragged food items out of the fridge until the bench was covered with them.

There was no point in dwelling on any of this. Soph started to mix ingredients.

'The ankle is improved enough that the physio says I can ease back on the exercises. The ones he still wants done, I can manage on my own.' Grey was in the living room. Soph had joined him there and asked if he needed to exercise his ankle.

Her mouth pursed and she nodded. She had Alfie the rabbit on her lap and she stroked his fur absently. 'That's good news. At this rate you'll be better in no time.'

Grey had looked forward to the day that would be the case. He hated the restrictions, the need for someone else to drive him places, all the things that impeded him. He wanted to have Soph's touch on his arm and be able to close his fingers over hers with his other hand. But that wasn't going to happen, whether he had the use of two arms or not.

And getting better would also mean Soph would leave. 'My blood pressure is also dropping, as are the other readings.' He growled the news.

She didn't seem to notice. Instead, she lowered the rabbit to the floor. 'Thank you for telling me. You'll be back working those long days and thriving on them before you know it.'

'That's right. It's what I want for my life.' Actually, the doctor had warned him about that, had said he couldn't just go back to the way things had been.

They had argued almost nose to nose until Grey had realised he was being a horse's rear and had apologised. Then the doc had suggested he figure out some way to realign his working life and his attitude overall.

Try trusting the people around you a little, the doctor had said. *You might be surprised how easy it is to take a more balanced outlook to your work and life.*

Grey had attempted to recuperate from the conversation by visiting his company. He'd spent three hours there before Leanna had collected him and returned him to his house. She hadn't seemed to mind his silence, had said rather wistfully that it might be nice to have satisfying work to fill her days.

That was the thing—Grey did like his work. The doctor wanted him to take a whole new attitude towards it, not simply ease back for a short time and then dive back in as before.

Yet when Grey had stepped into his office and tossed out a rapid-fire list of things he wanted—reports and information and the latest on what was happening—and his assistant had fired right back with even more stuff, all he could think of was Soph summing it up as 'Everything's fine' and suggesting he say 'Good' in response and leave it at that.

He'd walked out before half the reports had come in.

He wasn't sure if he actually cared.

Soph watched the expressions pass across Grey's face and knew in her heart that they couldn't go on this way. Maybe they didn't have to. Maybe it would be better if she were to leave.

Perhaps she'd already known it, deep down, when she'd cooked all those meals and frozen them so it would be easy for him to eat well until he could get the cast off his arm.

He could do his physio without her, would obviously now start to spend at least part of each day at his office. His stepmothers were aching to have a chance to be part of his life. Providing that little bit of extra care he needed just now might be exactly the ticket for them to achieve that.

Her heart hurt as she accepted it. She needed to go. It would be best for both of them now. 'A lot has changed for you even in the last few days. I think I should—'

The ringing of her cellphone in her bag stopped her before she could finish the words.

Grey was glaring at her, eyebrows drawn down, his fingers curled where his hand rested on his knee. 'You should what?'

But she turned aside, reached for her tote bag and drew her cellphone out of it. 'I'm sorry. If it's a call from Bella or Chrissy I don't want to ignore it.' She flipped the phone open and spoke her name before Grey could say anything further. 'Sophia Gable.'

'Oh, thank goodness you answered.' It was her landlady. She was panicky and upset and her words spilled over each other so fast that, for a moment, Soph didn't comprehend the shock of what she was saying.

But it sank in, and she gripped the phone tighter. 'Are you certain? We haven't heard from them since the day they left.'

'Yes, dear, I'm certain. They demanded I give them contact details for your sisters, and that I get Bella and Chrissy to your flat.' She paused to draw a worried breath. 'When I said you should be the one to impart any information, they became quite angry.'

'I'm sorry you had to deal with that.' Soph tried to keep her tone gentle so she didn't upset the older woman, but her heart was pounding in her chest and her palms felt clammy and cold while her mind raced madly, trying to understand.

Grey was watching her. His expression was tight

and concerned and she had to look away because she loved him and this was too much.

'I'll get a taxi and come right now. Just keep your door closed. I'll deal with them.' She would deal with the parents who had walked out on her and her sisters and now were back, demanding to see Chrissy and Bella and…what?

'I can call your sisters—' her landlady started.

'No, don't call Bella or Chrissy. There's no reason they should be upset.' Then, fiercely, 'I can handle this. I want to do it. It's my turn to be the one to carry the load.'

She ended the call and hit speed dial for a taxi. 'Yes, a taxi, please, as fast as you can.' She gave the address. 'It's urgent.'

'What's happened?' Grey was on his feet.

Soph didn't know when she had stood, but she stared at him blankly until she finally said around a choked sound that was half laugh, half shock, 'My parents have returned to Australia. They want to see Chrissy and Bella. Something to do with work connections. It didn't make a lot of sense.

'They're very committed to their working lives.' She added the latter almost as an afterthought, but she remembered well enough how her parents' lives had centred on their careers and advancements to the exclusion of everything. 'I have to go. I want to be ready when the taxi gets here.'

Soph would have bolted outside, but Grey stepped forward and laid his hand on her arm. 'I'll come with you.'

'No, this is my problem. I don't want any help. I'll handle it on my own.' She couldn't let Grey help her because just being near him made her want to weep. And she had to protect her sisters, and that meant leaving right now, alone.

A horn sounded outside and she snatched up her tote bag and rushed for the door. 'I—I have to go. My landlady let them into the flat. It's not her fault. She didn't know what else to do.'

Soph hurried on to the street, climbed into the cab and gave the address of her flat.

She was about to confront the two people in the world she had never expected to see again.

'I didn't know what to do.' Soph's landlady met her as she climbed out of the taxi. 'They were so demanding.'

Soph squeezed her landlady's hand. 'Please don't worry. Why don't you go back inside and make yourself a cup of tea and have a sit down? There's nothing to worry about. I'll attend to this.'

Somehow she would, and then…

Soph didn't let herself think any further. She couldn't right now. One emotional overload at a time, and she did feel overloaded. Would her parents want reconciliation? Truly Soph had never expected to see them again.

You heard what your landlady said. They want something from your sisters.

That might not be the case, though. Perhaps they wanted to reconnect and that had just come out because they felt nervous…

There was only one way to find out. Heart pounding, chest so tight she struggled to draw each breath, Soph finished climbing the steps to her flat.

For a moment at the top she hesitated, and almost turned around and ran back down again. But the front door stood ajar and she pulled her determination around her and stepped inside.

A car door slammed on the street below, but Soph's focus was all on the couple who sat side by side on her sofa. They rose as she walked in and the only thought she could manage was: *They look older.*

Then she unfroze enough to add more thoughts. They looked like strangers. They weren't smiling. There were no opened arms or stumbling apologies.

'Sophia.' Her name sounded alien on her mother's lips. She would rather hear Grey say it.

Soph pushed that thought aside. The stairs creaked outside and her heartbeat was loud in the silence inside her mind.

Why didn't she feel something—anger, betrayal, even the glimmer of hope that somehow they were truly back and all their lives could be rebuilt together?

Because you know in your heart that's not what they want. Look at them. There's no affection in their eyes. There never has been and that hasn't changed.

Grey's stepmothers had tried to hide their feelings, but the feelings had been there nonetheless. Why did it all come back to Grey?

Because you love him, and you wish you didn't and you're not sure you can make it stop.

'Why are you here?' Her words were so low, so tight, she wasn't sure they had heard her. Feelings did rise then, as she realised she *had* wanted something—a change, some emotion from the people who had brought her and her sisters into the world and then left them.

'If you've come to hurt my sisters…' They didn't want to beg forgiveness—that was clear. Soph would hurt about that later, but only a little. *Only a little.*

'We've come to see them.' Her father's sherry-brown eyes looked into hers without showing any sign of actually *seeing*.

'To see Bella, who was eighteen years old when you left? And Chrissy and I, who were still schoolgirls?' Three terrified girls. The words wouldn't stop. 'Bella lost her youth when you left us. She can't ever get that back. You both made that happen.'

'She was perfectly capable.' Her mother folded

her arms. She was still trim, with the same bone structure that had helped Bella make a success of modelling. She turned to her husband. 'I told you it would be a mistake to come here. We cut ties…'

Behind them, someone made a low sound and stepped into the room. Soph swung around and stared blankly for a moment until Grey came forward. He clasped her hand briefly and then stood there, his shoulder pressed to hers.

Comfort and warmth and sweetness flowed into her from that touch, and Soph marvelled that it could be so with all that was between them, but it was, and she let herself take it and stiffened her spine.

'Who are you?' her father asked as though he had some right.

'I'm Sophia's friend.' Grey gave it as much bear growl as he had ever done. 'And the man who can't believe you left her and her sisters.'

'We don't want—' Soph's mother cut her words off. 'We've come to see Arabella and Christianna. If that isn't possible today, then we at least want contact details. They weren't in the phone book under their maiden names.'

She made a frustrated motion with one slender hand. 'One member on the Board who must agree to employ us has met Arabella. The woman asked if there was a relationship, mumbled something about a fashion show and designer clothes and jewellery. She wants to meet Arabella's husband, and Chrissy's. She's holding out about our contract. We had to be in Melbourne today, anyway…'

It all made sense then. They had found Soph because she still went by the name of Gable. They didn't even know who Bella and Chrissy had married, and they could have found out, checked newspaper records, if they'd been prepared to invest any effort rather than expecting life to come to them, as usual. It was so…sad.

Grey gripped Soph's arm again. 'Let me see these people out. They're hurting you.'

The pain was in his gaze, buried deep in his eyes—for her, and for Chrissy and Bella. She shook her head and wanted to press into his side, turn her face into his chest and forget all this.

Be strong. You have to be strong.

She turned back to her parents. 'It's up to Bella and Chrissy to decide whether they want to see you.' She wouldn't arbitrarily decide for them, though a part of her wanted to. 'Give me your contact details. I will pass them on.'

Her mother opened her shoulder bag and reached inside. 'How do we know you'll do that?'

'Because she said so. Because she's your bloody daughter, in case you've *completely* forgotten that.' Grey stalked to the doorway and stood there menacingly.

'I don't feel like I am, though.' Soph searched both their faces one last time. Tipped her head to the side. She saw Bella in her mother's slender lines, Chrissy in the shape of her father's nose, herself in the colour of his eyes.

But these were just things, genetic markers. Soph drew a deep breath and let it out again and, unbelievably, found a smile. 'I don't feel like a daughter, but I know what I am. I'm a sister and a sister-in-law, an aunt and an honorary granddaughter-in-law. A friend and an employee and a rabbit owner. Those are the things that I am and, you know, it's all right. It's totally and completely all right.'

'I guess we're a little late. It seems our sister has said all that needed to be said.' Bella stepped into the room. Chrissy entered behind her.

CHAPTER FOURTEEN

WHAT were her sisters doing here? Soph frowned and didn't comprehend until she glanced at Grey and saw the answer in his eyes.

His mouth tightened. 'I know you wanted to do this alone but how could I let you? And I didn't know if I'd be enough.'

A chunk of her heart shattered into little pieces because he was *kind*, and *good*, even as he kept her locked out of his heart.

You would always be enough, if you wanted *to be*.

Their parents were putting their case to Bella and Chrissy. Though Chrissy looked ready to explode and Bella looked as coldly angry as their mother simply looked cold, Soph's eldest sister merely raised a hand to stop their flow of words. 'Leave your card. My sisters and I will discuss your proposal jointly, as we've done with every issue we've faced since the day you abandoned all of us.'

Their mother frowned. 'That doesn't suit—'

'They're not going to listen. We'll find some other way. I expected some maturity…' Their father took his wife by the arm and drew her towards the door. She hesitated and then dropped the business card into Bella's hand on the way past.

Not another word was said. Not even a final goodbye.

And then they were gone. Grey drew a shuddery breath and slapped the door shut, and for a long moment they all stared at each other.

Then Bella tossed the business card on to the coffee table. She held out her arms and Soph rushed into them. With a stifled sob, Soph pressed her head to Bella's chest as she had when she'd still been in school uniform and scared so silly she couldn't speak. 'It was my turn to bear it, Bella. I've never done enough, and they were so *horrid*. Why couldn't they just have wanted to *see* you and Chrissy?'

'And *you*, Soph.' Grey's voice was fierce as he said it.

Chrissy rushed forward and wrapped her arms around both her sisters. They stood there in the middle of the room, hugging, until Bella said, 'It's all right to cry. You can cry for yourselves, for us, but don't you dare shed a tear for them. They had all our tears…'

She couldn't go on and there were a few tears then, but they each heaved in deep, shuddery breaths moments later, wiped their eyes and separated.

'What can I do?' Grey's question turned all three heads, but it was Soph who couldn't drag her gaze away from him again.

His fists were clenched and his jaw looked ready to crack. She suspected he would agree to almost anything right now if he thought it would help them. Oh, God, she loved him so much, and he loved her. He did, somehow, to some degree, at least enough to feel this way, to want to protect her.

It's not the same. Don't fool yourself that it is.

'Maybe we should just go…now that they've left.' She didn't even know what she was saying.

Bella shook her head. 'Not just yet.' She turned to Grey. 'Thank you for calling Chrissy and me. You did the right thing and, if you wouldn't mind, maybe a pot of Chai tea? Soph will have everything you need in the kitchen.'

Her sisters had realised, of course. Grey's protectiveness—and, no doubt, all sorts of feelings parading across Soph's face too. If only they knew it was all totally hopeless.

Grey cast one sharp, protective glance towards Soph and then dipped his head and disappeared into the tiny kitchen.

Soph loved him for that too, for letting her have her sisters even as she ached for him and had to deny that ache.

Bella took her arm and gave it a gentle shake before she led her to the sofa and sat beside her.

Chrissy pulled the armchair close and sat down.

They left room for Grey on Soph's other side, a significance she didn't overlook.

'Do you have any idea how wrong it is to say you never did enough, Soph? Whatever has made you think that?' Bella chastised her and hugged her at the same time, and then sat back and waited.

'I was too young to do anything.' She had thought it didn't matter, that she had control of her feelings and had accepted that Bella and Chrissy hadn't asked more of her, but apparently it had stayed with her.

'We all did our part.' Bella squeezed her hand. 'All of us, Soph.' Her eyes filled again and she frowned and blinked the moisture away. 'I worked to earn enough money to feed and house us because that's what I could do. Chrissy finished her studies and then got a job because that was what she could do.'

'And I played with school friends on weekends and goofed off and spent more time begging you both to let me do your hair than I did on anything else.' How could that possibly be considered a contribution?

'You were happy.' Chrissy broke in with the words. 'Don't you see, Soph? Bella was terrified and I was almost as terrified and, when we both secretly thought it was all going to sink, you shared your beautiful loving heart and showed we weren't making so much of a mess after all.' A tear rolled down her face.

Soph reached for her sister's hand and held it against her cheek.

Bella nodded her agreement and her eyes darkened with remembrance. 'I kept things to myself. In trying to keep my own fears at bay I sometimes kept too tight a rein and didn't let you and Chrissy in as much as I could have.'

'You couldn't help that—' Chrissy started.

'I know.' Bella held up her hand. 'We all did the best we could.' She turned to Soph and smiled. 'I remember your offers of help, Soph, and I could have given you more responsibility. The truth is I needed your joy and your happiness and your freedom. I didn't want to do anything that might take that away. There were days when your smile and the knowledge that you were happy kept me going.'

'You're saying that was my contribution.' Soph was stunned, but the memories were there, tucked away—Bella's smiles, Chrissy's laughter as Soph had done insane things with her hair.

Bella nodded. 'Yes.'

Grey came to the edge of the room, teapot and cups on a tray. 'Soph?'

Just her name, softly spoken, and she wanted to cry all over again.

'Thanks.' She swallowed hard. 'Thanks for the tea.' *And for your care, even if it hurts to receive it.*

He sat beside her, his big body tense, protectiveness rolling off him in waves.

Bella poured the tea and passed the cups around. 'I'm going to drink this in one gulp, I think. It's been that sort of day.'

The sisters all laughed a little then, a release of tension, and Grey made a huge growly noise in his throat and managed to wedge his body half behind hers so his chest cradled her shoulder as they sat there.

'I realise I'm intruding.' Grey spoke the words with his gaze on Soph's face. He seemed to be asking what she wanted him to do, but telling her he wanted to stay…

Soph wanted him to stay, but this was sympathy, so *she* would leave *him*, as she had decided she must. Her mouth trembled.

Bella said quietly, 'This was unexpected, but there's nothing much else that needs to be said and I imagine this is a working day for Soph when all is said and done.'

'It is, but if Sophia can't cope…'

'I'm fine.' Soph's spine straightened. She *could* cope. She could leave him with dignity too, though she might need a chance to separate herself a little from this afternoon's emotional impact first.

Bella watched her thoughtfully but, in the end, nodded and sipped her tea.

Chrissy set her cup down. 'I'm sad for them. They really don't understand what love and family is about.'

'They wanted to use you and Bella.' Soph had to make sure her sisters understood that. 'I don't believe they'd have sought any of us out if it wasn't for that woman attending one of Bella's fashion shows.'

'It impacted on their career possibilities.' Chrissy paused to think for a moment. 'That's really kind of crazy, isn't it?'

'We did our best to leave the past behind and make new lives for ourselves.' Bella set her empty cup aside. 'In a way, this situation has given us a chance for a greater closure. We've seen them now, adult to adult. We've answered the question that maybe stayed hidden just a little in all of our hearts. Would they come back? Would they realise what they'd lost and try to regain it?'

'It wasn't like that, though.' Soph toyed with the rim of her cup while she fought a war between her conscience and a natural feeling of rejection. Her conscience won, perhaps by no more than a flicker. 'Bella's right. This is our chance to tie the loose ends. I think we should do it by inviting them to family counseling—a formal opportunity for all of us to address their past behaviour.'

It was a radical suggestion, but her sisters both slowly nodded.

'I don't believe they'll accept the invitation.' Chrissy pursed her lips.

Bella gave a thoughtful dip of her head. 'I don't believe it either, but it gives them a chance to own their past actions. We should do it through a solicitor, have him send a letter. We'll have the letter delivered so we know they get it. And we'll give our parents two weeks to respond. I see no reason to drag it out.'

No, they would all want to get on with their lives. Soph got to her feet and quickly cleared away the teapot and cups, washed them and set them on the draining board to air dry. With this plan in train, she felt marginally better.

They all moved to the door. Chrissy paused and smiled, with the first sign of humour since this had started. 'Nate will be surprised when I tell him what he's missed on his business trip.'

'I know exactly how Luchino will react.' Bella straightened the silk scarf around her throat. 'I believe there'll be some swearing and threats to rip our parents apart if they so much as upset us even slightly more than this. He'll be home from the auction tonight. I must make sure to tell him when Grace isn't in the room. She doesn't need a story about her father going ballistic to tell her school friends.'

They hugged and her sisters left. Soph felt a little

forlorn, but it had been a tough afternoon; she was probably entitled. Now she had to get back to the rest of the difficult stuff. 'Let me call a taxi and lock up. I'd like to just quickly check on my landlady and then we can leave.'

Though Grey still looked tense enough to snap, he nodded and waited for her to make the call, and then accompanied her while she reassured her landlady. It was a relief to climb into the taxi. 'I'll be pleased when our cars are returned to us. It's a nuisance having to do this all the time.'

'I meant to tell you. They'll be delivered tomorrow morning. I paid to get a transport truck through the lowest flooded area.' He paused and let his gaze drift to the window before he looked at her again. 'They'll bring all your things, and mine. I didn't want you to have to go without.'

'That was kind.' It shouldn't have made her emotional, but it did.

'Soph—' He reached for her, but she shook her head.

'You don't have to worry, Grey.' She could look after herself. She would survive her parents' unexpected appearance and ongoing lack of interest just as she would survive loving him. 'I'm fine. I promise you.'

She turned away so he wouldn't see the sheen of tears that came to her eyes, blinked until she got them under control and then kept looking out of the window because it was easier than looking at the man she loved and had to leave.

When her car arrived she would go.

Tomorrow… When she could do it and keep her chin up.

They went inside the house in silence. Grey cast one frustrated, tense glance at her and disappeared.

Soph took a deep breath and went into the kitchen, determined to get busy and stay busy.

Grey brought Alfie and plopped him into her arms, and then he just stood there in front of her and finally stroked her arm, just once, before he dropped his hand. 'Your strength and your giving attitude both humble me. I wish—I wish I could match those things.'

Her arms closed around Alfie and she hugged him close and let the feeling of his warmth and simple acceptance ease at least a little edge off her tension. 'You've reached out to Leanna—'

'Yes.' But his gaze told her he hadn't meant his relationship with his stepmothers, and Soph knew that, of course.

'We've both learned things since we met.' She had learned that when love came, a person couldn't do anything about it—couldn't shut it off or control it—and it just grew and grew until it took you over anyway, even when the person didn't love you back.

'I need to get on with dinner.' She sat Alfie on the

floor and pulled an edge of lettuce leaf out of the fridge and gave it to him, then turned to wash and dry her hands. 'I'm hungry, aren't you? I think I'll make three courses tonight. It will take time. You'll probably want to work in your study now you've got the all-clear to ease back into all that.'

It was a dismissal, clear and simple, and she was doing it to him in his own home, as his employee. She prayed he would let her, because all she wanted was to burst into tears and throw herself at him and beg him to love her the way she loved him. And Soph couldn't do that, couldn't let him see even a hint of what she was feeling.

'I'll go, then.' He hadn't wanted to.

She'd seen the resistance and, yes, the pain for her in his eyes. But he did go.

Soph set about making the best, most interesting meal yet, refusing to think about the fact that it would be one of the last they shared.

The cars arrived just as they finished eating breakfast the next morning. Soph drew a deep breath as Grey stepped outside to complete the transaction with the delivery people. She lifted the phone extension in the kitchen and dialled the number of the employment agency.

She threw herself on the mercy of the recruitment supervisor. She had thought she might get struck from their books, or at least have a lot of trouble acquiring further positions. But fate intervened by way of an urgent and last-minute need.

'I hadn't thought to go back into hairdressing but yes, I'll take it and, I promise you, nothing like this will happen again.' She had cited personal reasons but had not explained them.

If the woman on the other end of the line guessed, she kept her thoughts to herself. 'You'll need to be at the wharf no later than three hours from now. Can you do it?'

'Yes.' Soph drew a deep breath and squared her shoulders. She would have to ask Bella to take Alfie for her, drop him off, drive her car to her flat and then pack and get a taxi on from there. 'I can do it.'

She had to, because she couldn't stay with Grey any longer, and her courage now was as good as it was going to get to say goodbye.

When Grey stepped into his house twenty minutes later, Soph met him at the door. He'd heard her go to her car, but he'd had his back turned, speaking with the delivery people. He'd assumed she had taken some of her things out of her car as the keys had still been in the ignition, the doors unlocked.

It hit him now that she wasn't unloading her belongings. She had Alfie in his basket in her arms, a small travel bag and her tote bag slung over her shoulder.

Before he could do more than register the hard lump that had formed in his stomach, she drew a deep breath and spoke. 'I've taken another job with the agency. It's an urgent one, last-minute. They can't do without me and the truth is, you really don't need help any more. You're doing so well, so there's no reason I shouldn't go early.'

'You didn't mention anything.' It was all he could think to say. He felt stunned, shaken, and…he didn't know how to fix this. 'You can't go. Your contract here isn't over. I still need you.'

He needed to hold her because the pain she'd faced yesterday had nearly killed him but she had locked him out of it. He needed more time…

'No, you don't need me, Grey.' The words seemed to hurt her, but she tipped up her chin and forced her lips into a smile. 'You have Leanna, Dawn and Sharon to help you get around until you're fully fit again. They'll jump at the chance to be there for you if you'll just let them, and you'll be busy reclaiming your place at work.'

He shook his head, and she tightened her lips and stepped towards the open door. 'This is best. We got too close and that wasn't a good idea, and now we have to make a clean break of it, you know. Please, let me go.'

It was the heartbreak in her words that silenced him, and in that silence she walked away, loaded the rabbit into her car and drove off.

CHAPTER FIFTEEN

'THE agency has another project for you. It's of the highest priority.' Over the phone, the supervisor seemed to hesitate for a moment before she went on in a softer, less demanding tone. 'Arrangements have been made to take you to your next employer. I'm afraid you won't have a chance to go home first. If you make your way to the public transport area, a car will be waiting to collect you.'

Soph was almost there now. Her cellphone had rung as she'd headed in search of a taxi. Her stint on the cruise ship was over. She was tanned, rested and healthy and had done a wonderful job filling in as a last-minute hair stylist.

She had no idea what she wanted to do with her career path or her future generally, and she was utterly miserable. She had planned to go to her flat and collapse into bed for at least a day, and then maybe crawl out again to go and get Alfie from her sister's place before she talked to the agency about possible future assignments.

But she owed this supervisor, so she straightened her drooping shoulders and agreed. 'I'll go straight away. Is it here in Melbourne somewhere?'

'No, you'll be travelling out of the city.'

'Well, I guess that will be fine.' Maybe it would be easier not to think about Grey if she wasn't here. Not that being out of Melbourne had stopped her so far, but it would probably be even worse if she stayed in the city, so close to him. No doubt Bella would agree to keep Alfie a bit longer, though Soph had really missed her pet.

She glanced up. 'Ah, there's a man with my name on a placard over there. I guess I've found my lift.'

The supervisor seemed pleased to end the call. Soph realised too late that she hadn't received any instructions really, but it would have to wait now. The man was already taking her bags from her and hustling her into his car.

He drove without speaking, though he cast the occasional curious glance her way.

She was deposited beside a helicopter before she could blink. Well, virtually. She'd forgotten to ring Bella. She would have to contact her sister later.

The driver handed her luggage to the pilot and the pilot helped her into the helicopter and then they were off. It all felt a bit surreal and Soph still just wanted to close her eyes and stop thinking and not start again until she could do it without aching for Grey.

Four weeks on a cruise ship seeing the most beautiful islands and ocean imaginable, and she hadn't managed to forget him in the slightest. She stared morosely out of the window without really seeing anything.

'We've set down, love.' The pilot's words impinged on her bleak thoughts.

'Oh. Yes.' She turned to stare at him blankly. 'Thank you. I'll just get my bags, then.'

But he got them organised for her and, by the time she'd climbed out, they were waiting for her and the helicopter had lifted off and there she was, in the middle of a meadow.

A meadow full of spring flowers, deeper into bloom than before, all that excess water dried up and disappeared, but, oh, she recognised this place.

'I was afraid you wouldn't come.' Grey came forward—no, he *strode* forward without any apparent ankle difficulty. He swung two healthy, unencumbered arms as he moved and came to a stop in front of her.

'You're the assignment who needs me?' She couldn't make sense of it, so she shook her head. 'Didn't you tell them? You can't want me.' *I can't be here. I can't do this again.*

'Would you mind very much if I needed you,

Sophia?' He asked it so sincerely and his eyes seemed to look so deep inside her, as though he needed an answer only she could give him, an answer to something more than the words that made up his question.

Her heart jumped and she wished that just once she could be stronger, could overcome these desperate feelings. It had all meant so much to her, but that didn't mean it had to him.

So maybe he just simply wanted help again and wanted her because…because he liked her cooking or he knew she could type or something. 'You need someone again? Is it to work here for you while you supervise the repairs to your house?'

'No, those have all been done.' He lifted her luggage and started to move away with it, back towards the house, and when he got there he climbed the veranda steps and set her things down outside the front door.

The vines about the veranda poles had tiny white flowers all over them. Soph stared at them and at the familiar house and remembered finding heaven in Grey's arms, and she fought to swallow over the emotion that clogged her throat.

Words choked out of her. 'I can't work for you again.' She wouldn't be able to hide her feelings. Now she was stranded here. Panic rose in her throat. 'The agency didn't explain it was you.

'I'll call one of my sisters. Get them to come and collect me. I can wait by the road and be gone before you know it. I'm sure the agency will find a suitable replacement when I explain things to them.'

Soph was over feeling bad about relying on her sisters. That was what family meant and it went both ways. She had come to terms with that much, at least, as her sisters had reported back to her while they'd gone through the process of offering their parents reconciliation, and had their offer ultimately ignored. Well, no surprises there, really, and it *had* only hurt a little—because they had done their grieving years ago.

'Would you mind if we talked first before you make any decisions about going? There are some things I want to tell you.' He moved down the veranda steps and away from the house. 'I thought we could go back to the meadow, to the spot we visited before. Now that my ankle is better and the cast is off my arm, I rather like to get out of doors and…I thought you might enjoy the flowers. They're bright and beautiful, in full bloom now.'

Her heart twisted. Grey had once said that he liked her brightness, but being liked wasn't enough. Maybe he felt things had ended abruptly when she'd left. If so, he deserved the right to say whatever he wanted to, she supposed.

'You're welcome to say anything that's on your

mind, but let me phone one of my sisters now so they can get started in their car.'

'Of course.' He didn't meet her gaze as she drew her cellphone from her bag.

It seemed wisest to try Bella, but Soph couldn't contact her at the shop or at home. She left messages and tried Chrissy but got the same result. It was a whole lot of bad luck, and Soph felt panicky again.

'Don't worry about it for now.' Grey made the suggestion in a gentle tone that was almost her undoing.

He took her arm and coaxed her into the middle of their meadow. No, it wasn't *their* meadow. It was a place where they happened to have had a picnic once.

But there was the same bright blanket and a basket exactly where they'd sat the last time. She almost turned and ran away.

He gestured towards the blanket. 'Will you sit with me a while?'

I would sit with you for ever, but you wouldn't want me to stay that long.

'As neither of my sisters appears to be around right now, I seem to have the time.' She curled up right at the edge of the blanket and waited for him to sit on the other side.

He moved the basket out of his way and sat beside her instead, and then turned to face her. 'I don't have the close relationship with my stepmothers that you have with your sisters.' For a moment he paused and seemed to be gathering his thoughts. 'Part of that is my fault because, after thinking they had each deserted me, I put up shields and refused to let them near again.'

'They do care about you.' She rushed to say it because it was so obvious to her. Because she wanted him to have a loving family and all the happiness he deserved, even if she couldn't be the one to give it to him, and she thought he had been on the way to that. 'Has something happened?'

'No. Only good things.' He cleared his throat. 'I care about them too. I'm trying to show them that now, and I've realised they've all been bored so we had a family council like you did with your sisters that day, and came up with a solution.'

She leaned forward, just a little, just because she was happy for him, happy he had hope about this aspect of his future. 'What is it?'

'I've asked them to set up and run a charitable arm of the company.' He leaned closer, until their thighs were almost touching, and she could hear the soft sigh of each breath he took. 'They've taken to the idea with enthusiasm. I think it's going to really change them, and they seem to want that, to be occupied, to have goals and responsibilities.'

'That's a wonderful idea.' Wonderful and generous, not only to others but to his stepmothers.

'I'm sure that feeling they're a part of your work will somehow draw them all closer to you.'

He dipped his head but seemed to have more he wanted to say. 'There are other people in the company who need to have that sense of fulfilment and achievement as well. I made that difficult for some of the more senior people because I insisted on controlling everything so tightly myself.'

'It's safe that way.' She had picked on him for it, had preached that he should give others a go.

But she wanted that same control in her private life. It was dangerous and painful to let it go, even a little. She had learned that and broken her heart in the process.

'It is safe. You're right.' The green of his eyes seemed to deepen as he gazed at her. 'But sometimes you have to do the thing that isn't safe. You have to commit to it, even when you don't know what the outcome will be.'

His face was a breath away from hers now. She forced herself to inhale slowly and prayed that her heart wasn't in her eyes.

His voice dipped to a deep rumble that poured over her skin and made her heart ache. 'I've made changes at work, have distributed responsibility more appropriately. I realised I can't control everything that happens in my life, yet even though I've dealt with these things, I can't feel free right now.'

'How can I help you?' How could she not ask him this? It hurt to love him. It hurt more to think that he was unhappy. 'Whatever it is you need. I'll stay and work for you again…'

Even though it would break her heart all over again, one small piece at a time.

His hands closed around hers and held tight, and his face clenched into sharp planes and angles as he took a deep, deep breath. 'I'm making a mess of this. I'm a little uncertain of my ground. I…haven't done anything like this before. I'm nervous, I suspect.'

Again she didn't understand, but the touch of his hands felt wonderful against hers and, for a moment, she let herself simply accept this one small token while she could.

'You don't get nervous, Grey.' Agitated, maybe, but not nervous. 'Not even when you could be about to lose millions of dollars.'

'There's something a lot more important than that at stake this time.' Something in the tone of his voice made her go completely still.

And Grey went on. '*I need you, Soph.* I need you to forget I've been an idiot and said all the wrong things and had you in my arms and been stupid enough to let you go.'

'What—what are you saying?' Her heart stopped completely and then tossed itself around inside her chest until she felt dizzy and had to suck in a hurried breath to try to steady herself. Was he asking her to renew their relationship? Asking for an affair?

She would say yes.

You can't say yes.

Soph opened her mouth, though she had no idea which response would emerge, but he held up his hand.

'I need you to give me another chance so I can find some way to convince you to love me, even just a little, and I'll love you enough for both of us and hope you come to love me more in time; just don't leave again.' His words ground to a stop and he said in a low, raw tone, 'I don't want you to ever leave.'

'Ever…' Oh, dear God. She wanted so desperately to believe he truly loved her and wanted her for ever.

How could she believe that? He may have changed his working life and rediscovered his family but how…?

'You don't want a picket fence.' He never had wanted that. 'You want your work and your challenges and women who'll be sophisticated in the morning, not bring you breakfast in bed because they don't know how else to pretend it doesn't matter. I don't even know what I want to do with my life, whether I want to go back to hairdressing…'

'I don't want anything or anyone but you.' His fingers came back to tangle with hers, and moved across the back of her hand in gentle strokes. His thigh pressed against hers and he inhaled deeply and went on. 'When we met I thought I wanted to live my life by myself, without the complications my father brought into all his relationships.

'I don't want that any more. I want happiness, with you. Whatever you do, however you spend your time. I'll support anything that makes you happy.' He swallowed and the mask of his unease fell away to reveal all his need for her.

'You truly love me?' Enough to set aside an attitude that had lasted most of his lifetime and reach for something entirely different with her? Enough to set aside his fears?

His mouth softened as he searched her face. 'I think I loved you the day I met you. I just couldn't see it for what it was at first.'

He came up on to his knees beside her and drew her up with him. 'I let you leave when I should have asked you to stay. Not because I needed your help. You were right about that—I was almost recovered by then, though Doc Cooper has finally got through to me and I've accepted I'll probably always have to watch certain things, maybe always be on blood pressure meds…'

He grimaced. 'Not so much of a bargain for you to take on, perhaps, but I need you. You, Soph, with your multicoloured hair and wild clothes and your innovative cooking and your adopt-a-rabbit schemes. I need you even though I'm flawed and far from perfect.'

She hardly dared to believe his words, but Grey was in earnest and her heart jumped, but she felt sick inside too. 'You're *not* far from perfect.'

He smiled and shook his head. 'I'm in love with you, Soph. I want it all with you—marriage, children—and I'll try to be a good husband and a good father if you'll help me to learn.' His chest rose and fell with deep, uneven breaths. 'I didn't have the best example but I was wrong to let that example cloud my life the way I did. I don't want to do that any more.'

'You didn't know what would happen if you had to trust someone to love you in that kind of relationship. It was natural to want to protect yourself.' Soph didn't know what would happen in that case.

She loved Grey, was madly *in love* with him. She was thrilled that he wanted to embrace love and commitment with her, and she was also…terrified.

'Soph?' He was waiting.

He needed her to say something. To say yes. She should say yes, and she wanted to say it, so why couldn't she force the words out?

'I love you. *I do.*' Somehow she was in his arms and he was holding her, but when he would have kissed her, she looked into his eyes instead and forced herself to admit what she had buried all this time, had blamed on others, ignored and pretended hadn't existed.

This was the sick feeling inside her. Now that she realised it, she didn't know if she had the strength to overcome those fears she had disguised in the name of not being ready, of not wanting to be too serious with a man.

How much more serious did it get than loving someone so much she didn't want to imagine her world without him in it?

'I thought I left because you couldn't love me, because you couldn't give me the kind of commitment I wanted.' Oh, it had been so easy to blame it all on him. 'I guess I did, but now that you've said you do love me, I have to trust that you mean it and you'll keep meaning it.'

He stroked his fingers through her hair. 'I'm not your parents. I'll never abandon you, Sophia. I was stupid and I made a mistake but I love you so much. I would rather die than hurt you.'

She looked into his eyes and she saw his protectiveness, the way it had grown.

He had growled and grumped his way through his injuries while she'd bossed him around and carted him all over the countryside and the city to keep him entertained.

They were so different in so many ways and she loved every difference and every way they complemented each other. She loved him, and she'd been foolish.

'I love you, Grey. I want to be with you for ever. I love you and…' she sucked in a deep breath '…if *you'll* help *me*, I want to trust you to love me back.'

With those words she opened her heart to him, to the future, and the last of her fears melted away.

'Soph.' He kissed her then, and she kissed him back while bees buzzed in the meadow and the flowers and grasses swayed in a light breeze all around them.

When the kiss finally ended she glanced at the unopened picnic basket beyond them.

He followed her gaze, smiled and held her against him with one arm while he tugged the basket forward with his free hand. 'It's not a meal. This was my box of tricks to help convince you of how much I wanted you to stay with me. I got so desperate I just begged instead.'

'You organised it so I'd be brought here. You must have done a lot of plotting.' She had realised it on some level, but it only really sank in now and a soft smile spread over her face because it was nice that he had tried so hard. 'I'm amazed my sisters let you.'

For of course she realised that now too. It explained her unanswered phone calls. Maybe it was not so amazing, because her sisters would have seen her love for him that day. If they had thought he returned it… 'What's in the basket? Tell me.'

A tinge of colour came into his cheeks, but he lifted the lid of the basket and drew out an enormous book and handed it to her.

Soph read out the title. *'The Great Big Massive Book of Every Food Ingredient Imaginable.'* She weighed the heavy volume in her hands. 'It certainly is big.'

'I bought it to show you that I adore your cooking. I'd like to share the book with you, take turns trying out fun ingredients and ideas…'

The commitment in his words filled her heart. His gaze darkened as he spoke it aloud. 'I want to spend the rest of my life eating with you, loving…'

'I think I'd like that very much.' Because her eyes were prickling and she thought she might melt in a puddle of tears all over him, she drew a trembling breath. 'Is there more?'

'Yes.' He handed her a book about rabbit breeding. 'If we're going to be a family, I think Alfie should have someone special, and I have no doubt that will lead to several someone specials quite quickly. At least this way we'll know what we're in for.'

Her eyes brimmed with tears and she swallowed hard. 'I'm sure Alfie will be touched that you thought of him.'

From the basket, Grey also brought out exotic oils. 'They're for the incense burner so you'll have the pleasure of scents all around you. At dinner. In the bath. Whenever we make love. I want very much to make love with you again, Sophia. There's some for massage because I really wanted your hands on me that day.'

'I—I want all of that too.' Soph tingled with anticipation and desire and love. She looked at him and realised breathlessly that they truly had a lifetime ahead of them, to love and make love and laugh and face whatever came, secure in each other. 'I love you so much.'

He caught his breath and reached inside the basket and brought out one last thing. A small, slim, embossed card. It bore the name and details of her brother-in-law Luc's jewellery store.

Soph looked at it blankly and then lifted her gaze to meet Grey's. His eyes had turned a deep emerald-green.

He cleared his throat. 'I think we should buy Montichelli engagement rings. It would only be fitting and, in any case, I want the best for you. And…uh…I hope you don't mind that I want us to pick them out together.'

He laid the card on top of the books and reached for her hand and held it. 'I want you to have a beautiful wedding, and diamond rings that reflect all the different colours you'll wear each day. I want you to wear blue or green or orange wash-out hair when we get married.'

The tears in her eyes touched her lashes and spilled over. 'Oh, Grey.'

'You're the colour and the beauty in my world,' he admitted, stroking the tears from her cheeks and kissing where they had been. 'I want that lovely wedding for you, but I can't wait that long to tell the world we belong to each other.'

'I'd really like to give you a ring. It could be a signet ring…' Then the significance of all he had said really hit her and she stilled and her eyes widened as she stared at him.

'Will you marry me, Sophia? It's what I've been trying to ask you.' His mouth curved up in a rueful, loving, half-pleading smile. 'Please, put me out of my misery and say yes.'

'Yes. Yes, I'll marry you.' She whispered the words and he snatched her into his arms.

The books and other things went flying and a moment later they were flat on the blanket with the blue sky above them, and he peppered her with kisses and laughed until she pushed him down and took her turn to kiss him.

And then they stilled and he stared deep into her eyes and love poured from his gaze to hers and she sent it back to him.

'I'll probably always growl,' the bear warned. 'In fact, I'm going to do it now.' Grey put on his growliest tone. *'Say yes again.'*

'You might growl, but I'll probably be a butterfly about work all my life, trying out new things all the time. And you may not have noticed, but I know how to get my own way.' She grinned at the mixture of love and humour that came to his face, and then her smile faded.

'Yes, Grey. I'll say it as many times as you want to hear it.' She let all her love shine for him from her heart and her spirit and her soul. 'Yes and yes and yes.'